IMAGINE THAT

A Small Town Big Love Novel

KELLY COLLINS

BOOK NOOK PRESS

CHAPTER ONE
Kevin

Kevin Hoisington's life began when Maya staggered past him nearly a year ago. She was a Blackwood by birth and kept her name after her marriage to Brad Dick. He couldn't say he blamed her.

When she arrived in town, she needed someone and he set out to make sure that someone was him. Checking on the welfare of the people who lived in Blackwood was his job, so he drove the town twice a day to make sure everyone was safe.

There was nothing like the serenity of a new day. The way the light painted the Rocky Mountains and put a sparkle on the frost of an early spring never got old. Blackwood was not much bigger than a shadow cast against the mountains by a cloud as it passed across the sun, but it was huge to him.

Everything he wanted was here, including Maya. As far as he was concerned, all was right with his world.

As he finished cruising the streets of humble homes he and the bartender Damon Perry called Blackwood's suburbia, his radio hissed, and he answered the call.

"This is Kevin."

"Kev, I have Maya Blackwood sitting at my counter," Damon said in a voice that was barely above a whisper.

No sooner had Damon entered his mind, he'd called. Life often worked that way. They'd been professional football players at different times and on different teams, but they worked out together. With so much in common, they'd become good friends. Kevin thought the bartender would make a great cop. He was an invaluable asset in situations like these.

Maybe thinking about Damon and Maya within minutes of each other had been a premonition of sorts.

When Damon said Maya was at the bar, Kevin's stomach dropped, taking his heart with it. The last place Maya needed to be was in a bar.

"On my way," he said, drawing in a deep breath.

He was just two turns from the Blackwood Saloon. Except for the asphalt paving, the building probably didn't look much different from when it was built over a hundred years prior. The cruiser's wheels crushed the loose gravel in the parking lot as he put the vehicle in park. He approached the front door which was unlocked, despite the bar being officially closed for business.

"Morning," Damon said, as he wiped down glasses and mugs.

There at the counter, quiet and contemplative looking, was the long and lean Maya Blackwood, of the same Blackwoods for whom the town was named. Every time he looked at her he thought "model-beautiful." He was probably the only person on the planet whose heartstrings pulled tight when she was around. A tug of love and sadness at the same time. Few people felt sorry for the billionaire heiress, but he did. He wasn't sure if he loved her yet—he was still sorting that out. There was a disconnect between his logical side—his head, and its emotional counterpart—his heart.

"Hey." He approached her with an easy, soft whisper. He didn't touch her. Didn't want to unsettle her, but he wanted to get close to her and figure out why she was sitting in a bar at the crack of dawn. "You okay?"

She shook her head, sending the long black curtain of her hair swinging across her back. "I woke up and felt alone." The sadness in her voice hung in the air. "There's nothing wrong I can put my finger on. I couldn't shake the urge. Damon was nice enough to let me in."

She sipped her ice water.

"Just waiting on a fresh pot of coffee," Damon interjected before moving to the other end of the counter to give them privacy.

Maya and Kevin lifted their heads at the same time and gazed into the mirror behind the bar. Kevin was struck by what a handsome couple they made, even though they were just friends. He rested his arm on the bar as he hovered behind her.

Though Maya was a tall woman, he was still a mountain of a man next to her. The sleeve of his uniform cut against his thick bicep, pulling at the cotton of his shirt. Having played three seasons for the Denver Broncos, he was forever doing battle to find the proper fit. Looking at Maya in the mirror, he thought there was nothing to tailor there, she was off the rack perfect for him.

"You've got a lot going on, Maya. A new way of life. A new home. It's a challenge getting used to new digs, even if that house is spectacular," he assured her. "Now that the town has been sold, things creep up on us and come out in the form of a desire to self-sabotage. Especially when you're new at this. You want a drink but you don't need one."

She stared into the mirror but her eyes were on him. "You know, John gave the house to you too." Her face brightened. "Move back in. There's room enough for both of us. We can be roomies again and I wouldn't be so lonely."

He smiled warmly, but knew his position was firm. There was no way he could subject himself to that kind of torture. He couldn't live under the same roof with a woman he was attracted to and pretend they were just buddies. It wouldn't work. He could not be her "roomie."

"Maya, that big mansion isn't for me. I have a comfortable home more suited to my style of living." Staying at his place helped set boundaries as far as his feelings for Maya were concerned. "I like my place." He let the lie slip from his lips. "It's better this way."

"It's not a mansion," she argued. "It's an A-frame log cabin."

He dropped his head and laughed.

"Just a simple four thousand square foot cabin," he replied with a smile.

"Please—" Her lower lip rolled out into a pout.

She knew if she asked enough, she might get him to say yes. She could probably get him to do anything. That's how weak his resolve was when it came to her.

"On another note," he continued, not addressing her pleas to move back into the house, "this is not the place to come when you feel you need a drink. Call your sponsor. You know the drill."

"She wasn't home." Maya drew jagged lines in the condensation of her glass. "She didn't answer. Maybe she's tired of me calling her."

"Then call me."

She lifted her eyes and connected with him. Her expression turned from downtrodden to hopeful.

"You aren't tired of me yet?" She turned her face so if he moved an inch, he could kiss her.

"No," he said. "I don't think that's possible. Come on. Let's take a ride into Idaho Springs, hit up a 12-step meeting."

Maya laughed and that warmed him to no end. He was happy he could brighten her mood.

"That wouldn't look good. Me showing up to a meeting in a cop car," she said playfully.

"It wouldn't be unheard of. Besides, you'd be gorgeous in anything, including a cop car."

She touched his arm tenderly. It struck him funny how a single innocent touch from her could ignite his entire body.

"I'll be fine." She glanced around the bar. "You're right, this was silly." She pushed her glass of water away.

"Are you feeling better, at least?"

"Yeah, there's a meeting at the town hall at noon. Besides, Clem is coming to town, so I won't be alone. He says he and Kaitlin are done for good, so maybe he'll share John's house with me, and I won't be so lonely."

Kevin knew he'd told her he couldn't stay with her, and yet he was filled with jealousy that Maya's brother might. If only he could crush this yearning in his gut. If only she knew his true feelings.

Clem being there should be a good thing, but what if it wasn't? With Clem there, Maya might not need him. Her big brother would wonder why Kevin was always hovering around.

He silently scolded himself. This wasn't a time to be selfish. He was glad Maya Blackwood was sober, but the fact that she'd had a problem with alcohol at one time sort of put a wrench in the works, at least for the time being. Her immediate needs required him to be patient and not impulsive, but being around such a beautiful, engaging woman when he'd been alone for such a long time was a living hell.

CHAPTER TWO
Maya

"Good coffee." Maya took a sip and inhaled the steam rising from the cup. "Thank you."

"Any time," Damon replied.

"Can I have it to go?" Her eyes focused on the shelved liquor bottles. "I better hit the road before that Irish whiskey calls my name again."

"No problem." He transferred her coffee into a to-go cup, topped it off and handed it back.

She set a ten-dollar bill on the counter and walked with Kevin to her car. He was tall and solid and she liked the way he felt beside her. There was something they shared when he was near, some energy that crossed between them that pulsed deep in her soul. Maybe it was loneliness or need. Maybe it was love.

With him a step behind, she was tempted to stop and let

him run into her. Somehow, she was comforted by his touch, no matter how it happened.

"I'll follow you." He rubbed his boot on the slick asphalt. "I'm glad I happened by because I don't like you driving home alone on frosty roads when you're not a hundred percent."

His voice was always calm, unflappable, peaceful. Those qualities were alluring to her now that she was trying to repair her life from all the recent drama. Kevin was as warm and delicious as the coffee that Damon brewed, only he was sweeter.

"I never feel alone when you're around," she said with mild flirtation. "Maybe I had that in mind when I ventured out this morning. Maybe I hoped I'd run into you." She knew he didn't just happen by. Knew Damon would call him. Maybe she had banked on that.

"I'm glad it worked out." A smile brightened his face.

He opened her door and waited until she buckled up before he went to his cruiser.

Her Porsche rolled down Main Street to Interstate 70 with Kevin in her rearview mirror. She spied on him as often as she safely could, wondering if he was doing the same. Since she'd moved back to Blackwood, Kevin always made time for her, like now, driving away from town to make sure she got home safely.

They took the first exit, which led to a road that was nothing more than a long private drive to her cousin John's house. If they'd turned the other way, they would have run into her cousin Caleb's house, which was a twin of the house where she stayed. A drunk could get confused, considering there were only a few homes in the area.

She parked her Porsche in the garage but didn't close it. Kevin lingered on the driveway and rolled down his window. She never could seem to let him go. Nor could she tame the grin that always appeared when he was near.

"You wanna come in for breakfast before you drive all the way back?" Butterflies raced around her insides while she waited for an answer.

"It's not that far. While that sounds nice, I've got to get back to work."

The butterflies stopped and hurtled to the pit of her stomach where disappointment lived. "Okay." Her tone sank with her words. "I'll probably return to town around noon for a meeting."

"Be sure to stop by and say hi." He gave her one last look before he backed his SUV out and left.

She went back to bed. Or rather, she went back to the couch. When Kevin had shared the house with her, she had him move the comfortable sofa in the sparsely furnished home in front of the fireplace. She could spend hours staring at the flickering flames wondering how her life had taken such a sharp turn.

Today she looked at the empty fireplace and thought about Kevin. The heat of her attraction warmed her from the inside out. She tucked a throw around herself and sank into the best kind of peaceful sleep. A sleep that would start and end with thoughts of the sexy sheriff who'd stolen her heart.

When she woke, she freshened up to head back into town. She styled her hair just enough not to exceed casualness, but enough to be attractive. She put on the slightest bit of makeup so it wasn't obvious she was fixing herself up for him. Last, she put on a soft perfume that smelled of gardenias.

Under a blue Colorado sky, she drove toward town. It was funny how everything felt happy when the golden sun turned the cold frosty morning into a warm, sunny day.

Just before noon in a different mood and frame of mind than she had been in before the sun had risen, she moved toward the town, feeling enthusiastic and full of optimism.

She drove the one exit from the Blackwoods' private drive to the town center. At the end of the strip of turn-of-the-century shops was the town hall, where all the local functions were carried out. Why every meeting was held in room number eleven was anyone's guess. But its location was a bonus, being it was close to the police station where Kevin worked.

She enjoyed the hour-long AA meeting, grateful she didn't have to share that she'd had a slip that morning. She was happy to still be sober. When the hour was over, she snagged a cookie and a coffee from the table at the back and brought it to the police station, hoping to give it to Kevin.

She was filled with a burst of joy to see him at his desk. Had he just happened to be in while the meeting was going on? Often, he was all over the small town making sure everyone knew he was there and available.

She suspected he was at his desk while she was in the meeting on purpose—to check on her—but she didn't mind one bit. He'd helped to get her back on her feet. She wasn't sure if she would have succeeded without him.

She waited at the edge of his desk until he lifted his head.

"Here." She smiled as she presented the snack to him. "I stole these for you." She hoped the wink she gave him was sexy instead of silly.

"Are you ensnaring me with stolen property?"

Though joking, when he said things that way it felt like a mild flirtation. The way his eyes lifted, how his soft lips smiled—her body reacted to him as though it were. She stared at him with hope.

"Would it work?" She batted her lashes.

He laughed heartily while Maya melted. Her crush was growing roots. Kevin was, outside of her brother and her late husband, the most decent man she knew. He was warm and comfortable, and the fact that he was so incredibly handsome was a bonus she accepted gladly.

When Maya had lost her husband Brad in a freak accident on a mountain road, she thought she would die—or rather, she had no idea how she would live. And if she didn't die naturally, she was determined to help speed the inevitable along with alcohol and bad choices.

She had been on the road to self-destruction when her cousins John and Caleb, and her brother Clem voted to have her move into John's house so she could be away from the trouble she found in Idaho Springs. She took them up on it, but it felt like the proposition came with so much judgment from everyone but Kevin.

With the exception of the years he played ball, he'd been in Blackwood. Why he was still single was beyond her. He was extraordinarily handsome. What made him the perfect package was he was so attentive, loyal and patient.

He nurtured her along from those first dark days when she'd climbed out of a bottle. He was never intrusive or threatening. He never once hit on her, though she wasn't sure she liked that. She wondered if his kind and caring nature was part of him being an excellent public servant. Maya liked to test his will by flirting, but he never budged.

"Did you learn a lot at your meeting today?" He sat back and bit the edge of the cookie.

Their eyes connected and her insides quivered. There was no question about it, she had a huge infatuation with this man. It was good to feel something wonderful after only knowing grief for so long.

"I learned that I have the disease of self-centeredness." The corners of her lips stretched to greet her cheeks. "Which means all I ever think about is me. That's actually not true, so I'm thinking maybe I'm not an alcoholic."

Kevin flashed his bright perfect teeth. "You sure about that?"

She ignored his comment and leaned in for a better look. "Your parents spent a fortune on your teeth, didn't they?"

"Actually, I tried to bite a Raiders helmet and the NFL covered my costs."

"Raiders? Like the football team?" she asked excitedly.

He smiled again.

"No, like rogue pirates who pillage and plunder," he said with a wink. "Yes, silly. Like the football team, but my teeth came into contact with only one helmet."

"Where was I?" she asked, hanging on his every word.

Kevin got up and took a set of keys off the wall.

"I don't know where you were."

She considered all the years he could have known her and didn't. Maybe it was better that she'd been gone because it was all the past years that had molded him into the man he was today.

She laughed. "I hardly know where I was. My life has been a blur."

"If I knew, I probably would have been hurt a lot worse, because I would have been so distracted by you."

They both froze. He'd just openly flirted with her. There was no mistaking it. Half of her wanted to push it and ask him to have dinner with her. The other half didn't want to spoil it for fear she would chase him away.

"I have to go." He changed the subject abruptly. She didn't have to chase him away. He ran off on his own accord.

"Are you making rounds?"

"Doctors make rounds," he corrected her warmly. "I have a beat."

She followed him out of the station, tagging along like a puppy at his heels. That's what it felt like—puppy love.

When Kevin climbed into his vehicle, she walked down the street. Some of the other people from the meeting lingered nearby, talking on the sidewalk. It wasn't a gigantic meeting, though big for Blackwood, which said something for a town with only one bar.

She knew she should probably hang out with them and develop connections, but the better she felt, the less she wanted to. Meetings were great when she was at her worst, but as she recovered, she no longer felt the need to go. What she needed was to find something to do during the day. It was the boredom that was dangerous.

What she wanted to do was hang out with Kevin all day, but he took his job seriously, and she didn't want to become a pest. So far, he didn't seem to mind her being around. When her stomach grumbled, she glanced down the street to the diner.

With so many people about, parking was at a premium, so she left the Porsche in the tiny spot she'd carved out for herself.

She walked over to the Blackwood Diner and sat at the counter. A waitress immediately approached. Maya knew that it was probably because of who she was. She didn't like it that people thought they should treat her differently because she had money, but they did. She always got speedy, efficient service.

"Good afternoon," she said to the waitress. "I'd like a plate of fries, a side of coleslaw, and a job."

The waitress was writing until the last sentence, when she did a double take.

"What did you say?" she asked, squinting at her.

"I want a job," she declared proudly. "Are you hiring?"

Maya smiled and thought she sounded friendly, but whatever she said or how she said it earned her a scowl.

"They will tear down the town, you know that, right?" There was enough acid in the woman's voice to eat through metal. Never mind that her reply was more of an indictment than a question.

Clearly, the waitress was operating under a misunderstanding that she would straighten out.

"They're not tearing Blackwood down. They're giving it a facelift. This diner will still be here. Everyone will keep their jobs. I thought it would be nice to have one. Given the fact that the development company doesn't seem to be able to get their act together, that facelift might take a while."

"Is that so?" asked the waitress sharply. "Do you think it's cool for a wealthy person to take a paying job away from someone who might need it?"

Maya blinked. The reason the waitress jumped to wait on her was the same thing that made her think she could talk to Maya that way. She was clearly full of contempt.

"Pardon me?" She was stunned by the woman's mean words.

"I'll bring your order." She stomped toward the back to clip her slip in line with the others.

"I wasn't going to ask to be paid," she called out after the surly waitress. She fidgeted with her silverware, lining them up as if she were preparing for a dinner party "Do you treat everyone who earnestly wants a job this way?"

Suddenly, she felt like scrapping and apparently so did the waitress, who returned with a glower.

"No, just the ones who are rich enough to own a town. Have you ever worked a day in your life?" She fisted her hips and waited for an answer.

"I worked with an antique dealer for a while." It might not count as much of an answer, but Maya felt triumphant that she hadn't come up empty-handed.

"That answers why you sold the town. It was one big antiques deal," she said with a roll of her eyes.

"Did you get stiffed in that transaction?" She leaned forward. "As I recall, we signed some pretty hefty checks. Did you get paid?"

"I did, but some of us like to work."

"And you can't work?"

"Seems to be the case." She reached over and rearranged Maya's utensils, making sure the fork sat inappropriately next to the knife. "I know you say the people who bought the town can't get their act together, but they got it together enough to send me a pink slip."

Maya sat back, pushing the silverware aside. "That's not

supposed to happen. That wasn't part of the deal. Everyone should keep their jobs."

"I guess they don't want the likes of me in their fancy pretend Old West diner."

Just as she was going to ask the waitress for her contact information, a crowd arrived and took up the empty seats at the counter. She recognized many of them from the meeting. When the waitress approached them immediately, Maya felt dumb. She'd received no special treatment because she was a Blackwood. The waitress treated everyone exactly the same.

Waiting for her fries and coleslaw, she eavesdropped. The way they talked made it sound like they were all members of a 12-step group, the grumpy waitress included.

"Are you all friends?" She asked loudly.

They turned to her, saucer-eyed and silent. She extended her hand. "Maya," she said enthusiastically.

They each reluctantly shook her hand. It was clear she wasn't welcome, but she would push it anyway. Why not? She rarely fit in anywhere. She held her hand out for the waitress to shake. Now that she knew she was a member of her 12-step group, she would press her buttons for sure.

She moved closer so she would be part of the crowd, which was not as warm and welcoming as they were purported to be. She studied the waitress's name tag, which she hadn't bothered to check out before.

"You're Togi?" she asked with surprise.

"No, I just stole her name tag." Sarcasm floated heavy through the air.

"You're the fabled person they talk about in the rooms with a million years' sobriety, right?"

"Who You See Here. What You Hear Here. Let It Stay Here." Togi reminded her of the need for confidentiality.

"Wow, you're nothing in person like what I've heard," Maya said daringly.

It was suggested that members of the 12-step group be warm and engaging and these people were standoffish and cliquey. It turned her off big-time.

Togi's face reddened. She was an angry cork ready to pop.

"I wanted to ask if you'd be my sponsor?" It was a question asked on impulse.

The entire group made the same surprised facial expressions. Eyes large. Mouths agape. Heads cocked to the side in confusion.

Maya delighted in their shock.

"Just like that?" Togi asked incredulously. "Don't ask me."

"You have to say yes." She beamed with accomplishment. While not part of the actual constitution, it was an unwritten rule that people couldn't turn down service requests. She half wanted to dive into the program because people testified that it changed their lives, but then the other half of her wanted to expose them for the phonies she suspected they were.

"No, I don't have to say yes." Togi's expression slid into a frown.

Maya argued, playing a game. "Don't you? I mean, anyone

with your time must know something. Surely, you've got a lot to teach me."

Kevin walked into the diner and headed straight for her. He was so handsome, especially in his uniform. The way he moved made her rev from the inside out.

"Give me your keys," he said softly, without a care of interruption. "You're parked illegally. I've got to move your car."

"Ladies." He nodded to them in an old-fashioned, polite way.

"Hi," each of them said, studying the fact that she and Kevin were chummy.

She fished inside her purse for the keys.

"Jeez, Hoisington," said one of the women. "You don't move my car. You write me a damn ticket."

Togi's eyes narrowed.

"You serious about this?" Togi pointed between the two of them. "About working together? I'll do it if you are, but I'll treat you the same as anyone else."

"Yes," Maya responded, surprising herself. "I am serious."

Togi reached into Kevin's palm and snapped back the keys, handing them to her.

"Come back here after you move your own car and don't park illegally again."

Maya smiled and trotted out the door.

CHAPTER THREE

Kevin

Eyes narrowed and nose scrunched, Kevin took in the women sitting at the counter. They were like beta wolves seeking approval from their alpha Togi. Not sure about her, he stared her down. Why she cared if he moved Maya's car was beyond him but being questioned about it made his hackles rise.

"What?" she asked innocently.

"Is it okay with you if I go with her?" His voice dripped with sarcasm. "Or should I stay here?"

"Do you have a problem with letting her be responsible for herself?" asked Togi.

"No." He leaned against the counter. "I don't have a problem being nice to her either, which I suspect you might."

"How can you say that?" Togi's eyes flashed wide, no doubt taken from her arsenal of expressions she'd perfected as a drunk and mastered after she got sober. This one screamed victim.

He responded with a lecture.

"Because I know you." He held back nothing. "You like who you like, and you don't like who you don't like, and both decisions are made before you even meet a person. I can see it right now. You don't like her." He looked at the women in front of him and nodded at each as he moved down the row. "You should worry about whether any of you are likable. Maybe people would do you nice favors like moving your car if you were. When you don't get the same treatment as others, you need to ask yourself what you did to deserve different. Maya's only crime is being rich."

Kevin turned and headed to the door.

"She can do it herself," Togi called after him. "Part of recovery is being able to count on yourself. Promise you won't move her car."

He had a row of eyes staring him down, waiting for his answer.

"I won't," He said reluctantly. The truth was he'd do anything for Maya, but on this point Togi was right.

"All right then." Togi dismissed him and focused on her minions.

He walked faster to catch up with Maya. A smile on her face made her appear happier than he'd ever seen her. It was a far cry from that morning. Despite her back step, she was getting stronger every day.

He waited and watched as she backed her sportscar out of

the loading zone space. He waved at her, directing her to a legal spot.

"I'll stick out like a sore thumb." She spoke quietly over a lowered window. "Why can't I stay here? It's at the end of the street and no one's here."

He walked to the car and hovered over the door like he was making a traffic stop.

"Nobody can park if you're there. It's for loading and unloading."

"That's exactly what I'm doing. I'm unloading my body so it can load up on carbohydrates at the diner." Her grin was heart-stopping.

That damn smile could almost make him say yes to anything, but he'd never hear the end of it if he let it go, especially since he'd made such a big deal out of it in the first place.

"Do you want to report back to Togi that I let you slide?" His shoulders raised in question. "I don't. My coffee would never taste right again."

They lingered. He leaned on the car and stared down at her. He wanted her so badly. Those damn bedroom eyes that made his pulse race. Lips that were no doubt pillow soft and irresistible. Songs had been written about lips less perfect. If he leaned in and she moved toward him, their mouths could meet. But that wasn't the plan.

Kevin backed away from the Porsche so she could drive forward. She parked where she was supposed to and joined him.

"Are you telling me you're getting your coffee from another woman?" she flirted.

He wanted to grab her and kiss her, but he stood like a stone in front of her.

"You know she makes the coffee for the town hall meetings," he said. "Togi makes the coffee at the diner and then rolls it over on the cart to Room 11. In reality, even you're giving me coffee from another woman."

"I can't believe I've been plying your senses with another woman's wares."

He laughed and nodded. He thought she was adorable.

"It's not from the Blackwood Starbucks. But soon. Maybe after the development company rolls forward with the renovations."

"You know, Togi's going to be my new sponsor," Maya announced excitedly.

He stopped. "What? Was that what all that was about?"

"What?" she asked him.

"I don't want to interfere with your process, but she's prickly and not always friendly," he warned. "Is she the best choice? Where is your other sponsor? I thought you said you had one."

"She's AWOL or ignoring me." Maya let her shoulders fall forward. "I called her this morning before I got in my car and went for a drive. All I ever get is her answering machine. I heard her speak at a meeting once, and I thought she was awesome. She said she'd be my sponsor, and that's the last time I ever talked to her."

"You've been without a sponsor all this time?" he asked with one part alarm and two parts awe. Maya had been working her way through her sobriety without help.

"I haven't needed it. You've been a great support. My family, mostly, has been great too."

"Yes, but you know how it works. You go to meetings, get a sponsor, read all the books and stuff."

"And that's what I plan to do with Togi. She's got a million years under her belt. She has to know something."

"It's not a game," he said. "You share your deepest feelings and truths. This can get real and Togi can be cruel. I've seen her humiliate paying customers before."

"That's what she just did to me, but I put her on the spot. I asked her in front of people. She couldn't say no."

"Okay." He opened the door. "But I think you should pick someone nicer."

"It'll be fine. We'll focus on the things that people do when they get sober. I think this will be good for me. I want to see where it goes."

Maya was clearly excited to return to the crowd at the diner. He followed her inside, thinking he might join her for lunch.

He knew he would when he looked to the counter and found the klatch was gone—everyone—even Togi.

"Hey, where's Togi?" Kevin asked the line cook peeking out the window of the kitchen.

He had a sinking feeling Maya had been ditched, which sounded like typical Togi.

24

"Clocked out," replied the cook. "Gone for the day."

Maya staggered, her feelings clearly hurt. He knew given Maya's state of mind it was mean-spirited. He took hold of her hand and they sat in a booth.

"You were right." She let out an exasperated breath. "You said it wasn't a game and I admit, I did this half out of fun. We were playing a game of one-upmanship, and I guess she won. I got what I deserved." Each word was spoken softer until the last was a whisper. "I think I should leave."

"No," he said. "Breathe. We will walk through this together. Stay here and get something to eat. Have you had lunch?"

She shook her head and pressed her lips into a thin line. "I started this. I said I wanted a job and she made fun of me. I pushed it so she had to be nice. I guess I didn't push hard enough. People are so mean."

"They can be." His message was delivered with compassion. "Togi definitely can be, but people can also be good. Those are the ones you wanna focus on."

He rose from the booth and grabbed two menus then sat down again. He placed one in front of her. In through the door, Togi returned out of breath. Her arms overloaded with books, she slid into the seat next to Maya without asking.

"Did Arnie tell you I went to get my materials?" she asked, her face showing excitement.

"Hey Arnie," Kevin scolded in his sheriff's voice. "Did you forget something?"

Arnie palmed his head.

"My bad," said Arnie. "The books."

"Thanks for nothing," replied Kevin.

Togi studied Maya. If she was even remotely attuned, she'd notice the sadness in Maya's eyes.

"Did you think I abandoned you?"

Maya rolled her eyes and nodded her head, but she was too hurt to speak without a struggle.

"I don't know why I'm so emotional," she rasped. "It's so dumb."

"How much time have you got, honey?" she asked Maya.

Kevin was heartened by the fact she used a term of endearment. That was the signal that Togi would show her nice side.

"She has ten months," He answered for her.

Togi tilted her head. "Then what is she doing with you?" she half scolded Kevin. "You know the year rule."

"What?" He asked, red-faced. "She's not with me. We're friends, Togi. She's been going to meetings here since she got sober. How come this is the first time you've introduced yourself to her?"

He was hot. It took a lot to light his fire. He wouldn't put up with unkindness or innuendo. Fortunately, her remark about the two of them being an item went right by Maya, he thought. While it was his heart's desire to be with her, she needed nothing else to complicate her recovery.

"Yeah. We're just good friends," insisted Maya.

Togi looked at her the way a mother looks at a child. "I'll let you have lunch and then we have work to do."

Maya took a series of deep breaths and nodded.

"No matter what, I wouldn't do what you thought I did," assured Togi. "I know we sparred at first, but this is something I take seriously."

Maya lowered her head as if she were embarrassed. It killed him that she was feeling unhappy with herself. He had thought the same thing about Togi. He was pleased that he'd been wrong.

A new waitress approached. Maya kept her head down, pretending to read the menu.

Kevin ordered. "I'll have an unsweetened iced tea, Maya will have an Arnold Palmer and whatever Togi wants?"

"I'm gone," she said. "I wanted to give you your starter kit because something tells me you don't have one."

Maya lifted her head from the menu and smiled. "Thanks. You're right. I don't have a comprehensive starter kit. I have some of the books, but these are nice."

"Those were my sponsor's. She gave them to me." Togi set her hand on the stack of books and rubbed them reverently, like they were a treasure to behold.

"I'll give them back as soon as I get my own."

"These are yours. Just stay sober long enough so you can give them to someone you work with when the time comes to pay it forward."

"I like that." Maya stared at the books thoughtfully. "That's a nice idea and a good goal."

"Do you have time this evening? If so, we'll go to the eight o'clock here in Blackwood." Togi pointed out the window toward the town hall. "I don't have a car that will go much more than around here. Maybe one time we can go into Idaho Springs and hit a meeting. They have a good one tonight."

Kevin laughed and stared at Togi in surprise. "Have you ever seen Maya's car?"

"Can't say I have. What do you drive? A Tesla? A team of white horses?"

That made Maya laugh out loud, and once she started, she couldn't stop.

"She drives a Porsche."

"Figures." Togi rolled her eyes. "Looks like you're driving. I've never been in a Porsche." Maya's, shoulders rocked from her laughter. "I think someone needed a good laugh. We'll talk." She handed Maya a card with her contact information.

"You have cards?" He asked in surprise.

"You never know when someone will need you." Togi lifted from the table. "Take it easy, honey."

He watched Togi walk out of the diner, then turned his attention back to Maya. "That was a total surprise."

"It was," she replied. "You were right about her. She was mean at first. It bit me on the proverbial ass, but it turned out okay so far."

While he hated to extoll Togi's virtues, he had to admit that she had come through. "I thought she went out of her way to reassure you. But you aren't married to her as a sponsor. You can switch to someone else if it doesn't work out."

"How do you know everything?" Maya asked warmly.

"I just put things together." He raised his eyebrows. "I get around."

The waitress brought their drinks.

"I ordered fries and coleslaw." Maya voice barely hit a whisper. "It was a while ago so maybe they forgot about it."

The waitress named Kay lifted her eyes in surprise. "We didn't think that was a real order."

"Oh."

"No problem, though. I'll get it for you." The waitress pivoted on her loafers. "It won't take but a second."

"No, you were right the first time," Kevin said. "It's not a real order. Bring us a club sandwich. We'll split it and take two sides of fries."

When they had their privacy again, He pressed his reservations about Togi.

"Tell me why you want her to be your sponsor."

"Like I said, she has lots of time, and she will delight in telling me the truth."

"You're right on about that, but can you trust her?"

Maya looked him dead in the eye. "I have to trust someone. If she screws up everyone will know. This is a small town. She knows turnabout is fair play. Don't worry, I'll be fine."

He had said what he wanted to say. He knew he had to back off and mind his own business.

She touched his hand and changed the subject. Her fingers skated on top of his. It was the softest of touches, but all Kevin needed to make him hard. The damn woman could breeze past him and he was like a teen entering puberty.

"Do you know she said the development company fired all the employees here? As soon as they remodel, Togi and the rest are gone."

He wanted to reach out and stroke her hair. He loved that she showed concern for people who wouldn't give her a second thought.

"Doesn't sound self-centered to me," he said with a slight smile.

"I know, right?" She pulled her hand away and then waved it in the air in a what-the-hell gesture. "I'm telling you, I think I might have been misdiagnosed. I might not be an alcoholic," she said, making that joke again.

He wondered if she was trying to convince herself.

"Hey." His deep voice rumbled between them. "That's only funny once."

"I'm kidding," she insisted.

"I know, but just know that slips might start out this way. Denial works in sneaky ways. It's a good day now, but don't forget how it started."

She shook her head. Her face transformed with a brief darkness clouding her beautiful eyes.

"What happened, anyway?" Her fingers still sat on top on his hand, caressing the skin like a lover. "Bad dream?"

"Yeah." She moved her hand, picked up her napkin and frayed the edges. Tiny pieces of cotton-like paper littered the table. "I think so."

"Okay ... I wondered if you knew where it came from. Sometimes these things seem to show up out of nowhere, but they come from somewhere. Just pay attention. I've seen wonderful people who thought they had their problems licked go back to being worse than they were when they started."

"I got it, Kevin." Her voice tinged in irritation. "I have to stay on top of this thing. That's what I'm trying to do. Who knows how to pick the right person? I can't tell you why I want her, but I have a feeling about this. Togi and I might end up friends."

"That's a positive thought."

The waitress set their food down and was nice enough to split their lunch on two plates. Maya's phone dinged with an incoming text.

"Clem will stay for a few days." She set her phone down after reading it. "He's on his way."

"Good." Kevin nodded. "I don't like you being out there all by yourself."

"You can always move back in and share the house with me." She gave him a hopeful smile.

It would be comfortable and easy, but it would be wrong. Living with her would take advantage of Maya's vulnerability as a newly recovering person. Besides, it had been a long time since he'd been in a relationship. He missed everything about having someone. He enjoyed making her coffee in the morning. He loved sharing meals, but he had his own place and he couldn't stay at hers because each time he was there made him want her more.

He watched her deconstruct her sandwich and eat the parts one by one.

"What are you doing?"

He pulled the piece of bread she was about to bite away from her mouth.

"It's great together but sometimes it's nice to experience things alone. I'm savoring the small things in life, like how perfectly toasted this piece of bread is."

He cared for her more and more, constantly wondering if he wasn't, in fact, falling in love with her.

She set her toast aside and picked up her phone. "One more text and I'll put the phone away," she promised. "I'm letting Togi know I'll take her to Idaho Springs."

Kevin's chest was tight. Idaho Springs was connected to Blackwood by a winding mountain road. A road made more dangerous at night because of the dark and the wildlife that raced across the lanes.

He knew his possessiveness was ridiculous. It was what had run Lucy out of his life. If he didn't stop, he'd drive himself nuts. He wasn't Maya's husband or her father. He would lose her before he ever had her if he didn't watch his overprotective nature. He'd give changing her mind one last shot and then leave it alone.

"Is that such a good idea?" he asked. "That's kind of a trigger place for you. It's also a long time to be in a car with an iffy person."

"John, Clem, and you all thought it was a great idea for me to go to meetings. Now you're talking me out of them?" She huffed. "I'm getting involved. I'm not made of glass, you know."

Kevin spoke plainly to her. "You were in a bad way, Maya. You were gambling and drinking, not to mention being involved with the wrong people. The guy that Caleb found you with at the casino the night they took you to rehab had a criminal record. I'm just saying be careful."

Kevin tugged at his uniform collar, which seemed to constrict around his neck. He was off the clock at the top of the hour but for now, he'd straddle the line between friend and cop.

Blackwood had a police force of four, which meant they stayed busy. If they needed to—though they rarely did—they drew from surrounding areas, all part of Clear Creek County.

He'd been looking forward to getting a great night's sleep when he was off duty. Instead, he had a feeling he'd be going to Idaho Springs to keep Maya safe and sound.

He wanted to have a conversation with Togi about his concern for Maya, but that would tip his hand. He'd just come to terms with his feelings for the stubborn woman. He wasn't going to share them with everyone on the same day. If he didn't have to worry about her recovery, he would have made her his already—or at least tried. He knew that now. To hell with his possessive nature. Maya Blackwood was his. He took care of what was his.

33

CHAPTER FOUR

Maya

Maya drove back to her borrowed home with a full stomach and a need to nap. She'd had nearly no sleep the night before so the catnap she'd taken that morning after returning from the saloon only lasted her so long.

Could she sleep feeling so enthusiastic? It was clear it was time to do something with her life. Time to find a purpose and working with a sponsor felt like she was on the right track. Though it was silly to impulsively ask to work at the diner, she needed a job. Not for money but for self-preservation.

First, she had to deal with the loose ends of her prior life. The one she'd left behind. She needed to figure out what to do with the home she had in Aspen. When she became a widow, she drank hard and lived in the casinos in Idaho Springs so she wouldn't have to deal with the heartbreak of her lost dreams. A fairytale life that had died with her beautiful husband Brad.

She was grateful that her cousin John, who had just married and moved to Idaho Springs, had let her have his house. It allowed her to recover, but if she were honest, it also allowed her to put blinders on and not deal with what she had going on before she hit rock bottom.

Now that she was clear-headed, she wanted to take charge of her life. Couldn't wait for life to happen. Had to make it happen. High on her list besides her home in Aspen was to reach out to her family and their corporation to report that the development company they sold the town to wasn't keeping up with their end of the bargain.

She called her old sponsor and left a message to say thank you but told her she would move on. It was oddly exciting to commit to the 12-step program. Originally, she had gone to enough meetings to get her on track with sobriety. When she got enough clarity, it was a shock to reflect on how big a problem drinking had become. While in the middle of it, she didn't know when alcohol had become such a big part of everything she did, or how it had wiped out her life, but it had.

The other part of having something to do would keep her mind off of the fact that Kevin only liked her as a friend when it would be nice to have more. She had a fondness for him and made up reasons to be with him all the time. Hell, she put herself in his path constantly, and smiled and flirted, but he wasn't making a move.

He acted like he liked her. Clearly, he wasn't spending time with anyone else. He didn't seem to mind being with her but nothing happened. She replayed the way his muscles rippled when he'd risen from the booth at lunch to get menus. He was tall and handsome and big everywhere she could see. She was so drawn to him.

There was something—an invisible forcefield that kept her from full-blown hitting on him—though she reserved the right to try in the future. He was definitely sending her a 'friends only' message.

She regretted that she was just getting to know him despite being a member of the founding family of Black-wood. Private schools filled her youth, while he'd had a public education. They lived parallel and yet opposite lives. She didn't know who to ask to find out what his story was. He acted single, and yet it appeared he wasn't available. It made no sense to her.

Curled up on the couch, she flipped through some of the pages of the books Togi had given her. She texted a confirmation of her plans with Togi and then waited for her brother to come barreling in. She had a strong feeling it would be any second. She practically did a countdown on the couch, and sure enough, she heard the car door close, the footsteps on the gravel, and the key in the door. Every Black-wood had a key to everyone else's houses.

"Hey," she said casually.

"Hey back," he answered dejectedly.

Clem walked into the living room. He was shaggy and

thinner and obviously hadn't slept in a while if the dark circles under his eyes were a clue. Divorce didn't flatter him.

"I think I need sleep so I'm going to head for a bed. I'll talk to you later." He kissed her on the head.

She pointed to the western side of the house.

"Take any room on that side. The fridge is full. I'm going to make you a sandwich and leave it on the top shelf. You need to eat when you wake up. I'm going to a meeting tonight, so I might not be here when you get up, but I'll be home at a reasonable hour."

He stopped to study her. His star struck face brightened unexpectedly.

"What?" She touched her face, certain she'd grown a wart on her nose.

"You look great." His voice cracked with emotion.

He grabbed her and held her. Her face nuzzled against his chest.

"Jeez," she asked with a self-conscious smile. "Was I that bad?"

"You scared us," he said. "I guess I haven't seen you in a while. Your skin is clear. Your hair is shiny. I thought you would go bald it was so thin. You're still a string bean, but you're no longer a toothpick."

"I don't know if it's the sobriety or this guy I like." She hoped he'd ask her about Kevin.

Just thinking of him filled her with warmth and made her stomach flutter. She raised her eyebrows mischievously.

"You like someone?" he asked with a full-blown smile. "Why am I just hearing about this now?"

She waved off the topic like it was nothing. She wanted to say it was nothing. Had she been crushing on Kevin because he was a nice guy and she was misreading things?

"I probably shouldn't say anything. He doesn't know I like him."

"No, tell me." Clem sat on the armrest. "I have to hear."

"My reason for bringing him up is so you can see it gets better. All I'm saying, Clem, is this stuff with Kaitlin will pass." She closed her eyes and remembered her own painful past. "Brad was the love of my life. We were soul mates, and we had the whole picket fence plan. When he died, I never thought it was possible I could feel again. I'm feeling again. This thing with you and Kaitlin—"

He shuttered his eyes.

"I understand that. It's going to take its own time, but with all due respect, Brad didn't leave you because he wanted to. Kaitlin is leaving me on purpose. The hurt is a little different. Enough about me. Tell me about this guy so I have hope."

"It's an infatuation, but it's nice to have a thing that makes me feel happy. Something to look forward to."

"Is it a local guy?" he asked.

"Yep. No one rich or famous, though he played pro ball. It's the cop," she said. "The cop who has been such a friend while I get back on my feet. His name is Kevin. John introduced me to him. He shared the house with me for a while when I first got out of rehab."

"You lived together?"

"It wasn't like that. I guess he could have taken advantage of the situation, and I would have welcomed the diversion. I mean, how easy would it have been to jump into something to avoid walking through the pain of the mess I'd made of my life."

"Maya, it's understandable."

"You lost someone special and you didn't become a drunk." She regretted that she had fallen so low. Even though she had put her life back together, she was shamed by the choices she'd made.

"I've done some nutty stuff in the name of walking through this divorce." He laughed nervously. "I don't want to get into that. Tell me how he feels about you."

"He feels respectful," says Maya. "Thoughtful. Supportive. He wants to be friends. I don't think he likes me that way." She felt the pangs of crushing on Kevin as she spoke.

"What's not to like?" asked Clem. "You're gorgeous, and you're rich, I hear." He grabbed her like he would tickle her.

"He doesn't care so much about material things. At the end of my drinking, those blurry days at the casinos, I had one or two guys who found out I was an heiress, and they were my best friends." The memory was unpleasant.

"I was there and had to pry one guy out of your wallet. I thought I would go to jail for assault and battery because I was going to kick his ass. Glad you're not there anymore. You can't change the past, so don't waste your time trying. Pardon the vernacular. It's like pissing up a rope. Been there done that. I almost hung myself with it trying to make things be the way they can't. You can't undo what happened before you moved here. Just do the best you can now. If this cop is a good friend and that's all it is, well that ain't bad, either. We all need friends."

Her brother looked so tired. She hugged him again. He felt bony and thin. He was a bear of a man, to begin with, but he'd lost weight since his breakup.

"Go get sleep and then promise me you'll eat something." She tried to sound motherly and not naggy.

"Will do."

She watched him go upstairs. She would help him get back on track the way her family and Kevin helped her. But for now, she needed to work out. She headed to the gym in John's house.

Togi texted her. She accepted Maya's invitation to the meeting. That made Maya feel like she was heading in the right direction and she felt just a bit stronger. It also gave her a reason to text Kevin.

"Going to the Idaho Springs meeting tonight."

She dressed to work out. Most of the rooms in the house were high-ceilinged because of the pitch of the roof but she suspected John had them raised because the Blackwoods were tall people. John was the tallest at 6'4". Cousin Patrick was not as tall as John. Maya herself scraped 5'10." Clem was the next tallest male. Her cousin Caleb and her sister Jennifer were the shorties at 6'2" and 5'8" respectively. When they had a say in things, there was ample clearance.

John's gym was complete. It had a treadmill, a weight bench, a fully stocked weight rack, and a kick bag. It had a dance floor too so it was perfect for Maya's favorite exercise vice, the jump rope. She had a collection of ropes. She saw these guys on an internet video channel and she was hooked. It was the great part of addiction, which she only discovered after her beloved husband died, that if the obsession was to drink or gamble, she could focus it on exercise. In this case, jumping rope. She loved it. She cranked up the music on her iPhone and went for it.

It only took her fifteen minutes to knock out a set, then she rested and started again. As she finished her second set, she got a text from Kevin. She didn't read it, because if she did, she would ditch her workout. She was so hooked on jump rope and the high it gave her that she was torn between diving into a conversation and delaying that gratification for another time. She gave a quick response.

"Working out right now. We should do that together sometime," she wrote boldly.

Just like that, her life felt rich. It was such a different situation for a woman whose life, heart and soul had been shattered. And then it hit her. That's what it was. That was what put her in the seat at the saloon that morning. She had been disconnected from it or denied it. But now she knew.

It was coming up on Brad's birthday. His life was over far too soon. A sharp pain sliced through her right in the middle of the euphoria of jumping rope and the coziness of a crush and lay open a wall of sobs.

Seeing Clem and remembering why she had started drinking had just worked that sore to the surface. She pressed her face in her hands and cried, consciously sad for her husband in a way that numbing herself with drinking and gambling prevented. She wasn't sure how long she had been there. It felt like she was taking out the trash, she cried so hard.

Her tears unearthed months and months of stored grief that remained in her being and she had not processed. Just when she thought it was all gone, there was more. She felt a warm hand on her shoulder. No doubt Clem, who had come into the gym to ask her something and found her like this.

She rose blindly, allowing herself to be taken into his embrace. She felt the stiff texture of his uniform and realized she was hugging Kevin. The sequence was like a dream, she was so overwrought.

"What happened?" he whispered.

"How come you're here?" She pressed her head to his solid chest.

The release of pent-up grief left her exhausted. She was positively wiped out. He was so comfortable, she could fall asleep on him.

"I texted you that I was here and coming in." His voice had a soothing quality to it. "What's going on?"

"I figured it out, what got me squirrelly this morning. *Brad*," she whimpered.

He squeezed her tighter.

"There, there. That's normal."

Something about the way he said it, the way he felt, allowed her to let go more. Her body relaxed. Kevin's arms provided her with a safety net. She wiped her face quick-like and lifted it to him to kiss. His face fell before he stepped away.

"You're working out." He changed the subject.

Kevin had something he was dealing with or hiding. Every time they got close, he shifted gears. In her emotional state, it annoyed her.

"Kevin, how come you don't have a girlfriend?" She pulled no punches. Her question was direct and succinct.

The atmosphere in the room changed and he was quiet. Then he tried to laugh it off.

"Where did that come from?"

"I'm serious," she said. "Be straight with me. How come? You're wonderful. You're a good-looking guy. There should be a line of women offering to cook you dinner."

"I can cook for myself."

They stood in the middle of the gym surrounded by equipment, having this conversation. He took a deep breath. She had touched on something personal, a side of himself he didn't disclose too often, if ever.

"I had a thing for someone for a long time." He shrugged as if it wasn't important. "When I got over it, I realized it was a way for me not to be involved. In college and in the pros, I chased a bit, but that wasn't for me. I'm looking for the right one."

"I said girlfriend, but who do you have in your life? You take care of other people. Who do you have to care for you?"

He gave a sharp laugh.

"I have friends. You're my friend, silly. I consider Damon one of my best friends. I have family. My mom lives here. I have two sisters. They live in Denver. But I love the people of this tiny town. I grew up here. Blackwood is so small you see the same people day in and day out, you follow their lives and become a part of them."

"Our selling the town kind of changed that," she reflected out loud.

"Kind of." His tone was laced with uncharacteristic sarcasm. "One of my sisters, Kara, didn't understand why I didn't go the glitzy route when I played football. After she learned about the money they paid me, she wanted me to live in a house like this, with a trophy wife. This town is enough for me. In fact, it's the standard. I'll take a grumpy older waitress who probably should retire like Togi over the polished twenty-something they will replace her with."

"I missed all that." A huff of air left her chest in a whoosh. "This town bears my family name and I wasn't here for any of it. I would have loved to have been a part of something like that."

"You have a little while until the construction crews start rolling in and refurbishing everything to enjoy it."

"What did you stop by for?"

Kevin froze as if he had to scramble to make up an excuse.

"I'm anxious about you going into town. Idaho Springs is a slippery slope for you." He used the AA lingo Maya heard around the rooms. "It's full of gambling and drinking and dangerous characters."

"Togi will be my bodyguard. She's like a pit bull. If danger approaches, I'll let her loose."

CHAPTER FIVE

Kevin

Kevin left Maya even though he didn't want to. Holding her in his arms nearly crushed him. She felt amazing—her body was soft and voluptuous and warm, and the soft scent of her shampoo brushed his nose. He wanted to tell her how much he liked her—if like was even the right word because the moment he thought about it, it became so much more—but she was just getting on her feet.

He had one more drive-through of the town to do before wrapping things up for his shift. The mention of his mother prompted him to swing by and check in on her. He usually connected with her every two or three days. It wasn't like she was an old woman; she'd just scraped sixty.

She lived off of his late father's pension but worked at the nearest hospital because she wanted to. He felt the need to check in because she was by herself otherwise. When she met him at the door, something about her hair reminded him of Maya's and he rolled his eyes, because she also had something else in common with her. She was a recovering alcoholic. Franny took her meetings outside of town at the hospital where she worked and was truly anonymous.

"Ooh boy," he muttered as he compared the woman he had a thing for with his mother.

"Something wrong, dear?" she asked as she craned to kiss his cheek.

"No, I'm good."

"Want some dinner? I'll have it ready in a while."

Franny Hoisington was a petite, dark-haired woman. He got his light brown hair, huge frame, and height from his father. He was the spitting image of his dad.

"Yeah." He'd never been able to turn her down. "I will."

Compared to the sprawling Blackwood A frame that he'd camped out in for a few months after John moved to Idaho Springs, Kevin's house and his mother's house were far homier. When he stayed at John's house where Maya was now, it felt like he was at a ski lodge.

Every time he stepped foot in his mom's house—the house he'd grown up in—it felt like security and comfort. It hadn't always been like that. There had been a time when his dad was always out of the house and his mother was drinking.

He would come home from school and find her on the floor asleep. The house would smell of peppermint because his mother drank Schnapps. Even as a grown man, Kevin couldn't stand the taste of peppermint—not in gum, or chocolate, or even mouthwash.

Franny got sober when he was in the eighth grade. She was present for him during high school, college and while he played football in the pros. Something about the experience of having an alcoholic mom made him hesitant to connect on anything but a platonic basis. That turned him into a heck of a caretaker.

Having his mom be in recovery gave him a great resource to help the community when he needed to. It gave him insight with Maya, but now he felt like he'd painted himself into a corner. There were rules, and he wanted to break all of them.

He'd known from the moment he met her and knew of her situation that he would develop feelings. She was drop-dead gorgeous, a sweet and wonderfully honest woman who had lived through a tragedy. Maya Blackwood was made for him.

"I have to ask you to remember when you said there was a strong suggestion for newcomers—you know people who are newly sober? That they shouldn't get in relationships for the first year?"

"You mean like Maya Blackwood?" she asked without looking up from her saucepan.

"Yes, I mean her."

The mention of Maya by name made him warm and ache at the same time. He and his mother talked at length about her. He got a lot of advice because his mother was sober and worked with alcoholics. She gave Kevin insight about what Maya was going through as a person trying to recover from a tough stretch of drinking.

He'd known when he saw Maya for the first time she needed TLC, and that with help, she would become a remarkable woman. And she had. He found himself impatient for them to become something more.

"I think I might be in love with her," he confessed.

"You thought you were in love with Lucy Shoemaker," she said candidly. "That wasn't so long ago."

His mother, though great and approachable, was flawed, and she did the mother thing from time to time, especially with women. She had this way of throwing shade on the topic when it looked like he'd found someone. He didn't understand why.

"Mom," he argued. "That was over a year ago. Besides, she and John Blackwood are perfect for each other."

He was frustrated and felt like she was mocking him.

"Should I be getting advice from someone else? You don't have an ulterior motive here of steering me clear of women, do you?"

"No. I didn't mean that the way it sounded. It would be too selfish of me to interfere with you finding someone wonderful. I want to see you happy in the way you want to be. Isn't that Blackwood girl kind of flighty? Is she taking her recovery seriously? You might be in for some borrowed trouble."

"I think she's serious." Deep inside he knew that to be the

truth but this was Maya's journey and it would be a path full of hills and valleys. "I know she goes to meetings and she has a sponsor. And yes admittedly, she is a bit of a character, but I'm not into drama, and I wouldn't be attracted to her if I thought she would be a roller coaster ride."

"No one does life perfectly, present company excepted." She turned to him and winked. "Risk is okay, Kevin. She'll let you know if she's ready for something new. The thing about the first year is that while someone is vulnerable, they could turn to alcohol to cope. The truth is, as an alcoholic she could drink any time or not, but that is true for me too. We always have to be vigilant. It's all just one day at a time. That doesn't mean we can't live our lives."

"That's a yes?" His heart leaped for joy at his mother's support. "She doesn't have quite a year, but she's doing great."

"That's a be happy." She tapped the side of his head with her palm. "Quit being so damn careful. You're just like your father, thank God."

He wasn't sure what had just happened. She had given him mixed messages, but the last one was to give him her blessing to pursue Maya.

He followed her to the table. He felt like he had just eaten, but he'd only had half a meal since he'd shared his lunch with Maya.

Franny was an excellent cook. She favored whole foods, and organic ingredients so it wasn't like it was going to be bad for him. He felt a certain obligation to eat her food, but it was about time he had another woman besides his mother to take his meals with.

"Mom, can we have Maya over for dinner sometime?"

"Yes, I'd like that. I think it's high time. I would love to have a full dinner table. You say when."

"We can make it soon," he replied excitedly. "Whenever you're up to it."

"I eat every day, and now I am eager for you guys to come over."

"I'll let her know."

With that, He gave himself permission to consider going out with Maya. His head filled with thoughts of her. He wolfed down his food and washed his dishes.

"Hate to eat and run." He kissed her cheek. "Love you."

He jumped in the squad car and meandered the short distance to his place. He figured the eight o'clock meeting was about two hours away. He would meet her when she got out at nine. He could hardly wait to tell her how he felt. As long as there was no hard and fast rule about getting involved with her before she had a solid year under her belt, he wasn't going to wait any longer.

CHAPTER SIX

Maya

The sun had set on a long day. Springtime in Colorado was chilly but Maya sensed the difference between a winter chill and a spring one. It felt like spring when she left the house to drive to Blackwood, and that made her happy.

She spruced up to go to the meeting with Togi. It wasn't exactly like going to church, but she did put on fresh clothes and did her hair and makeup. She wanted to make a good impression for the newer people who might be at the meeting.

Her Porsche purred as it pulled in front of Togi's house. Somehow it seemed louder on the narrow, rustic streets. The glaring white European sports car was completely out of place in the working-class neighborhood.

It cost more than the houses set on the road and she felt obvious. Like so many of the homes that made up the residential portion of the tiny town, Togi's house was old but well-kept. It was hardly bigger than a boxcar but it was crisply painted and accessorized to undeniable cuteness. She felt a pang of envy for the quiet quaintness of Togi's world.

She got out of the Porsche like she was Togi's date, but the waitress was already out the door. Maya sat back down and waited. Togi got in the car. Her short red hair lifted in all directions by the slight breeze outside.

Togi wasn't big on making eye contact, though her green eyes were pretty. Maya took a deep breath, knowing this could be an interesting experiment.

"Good evening." Though Maya was nervous, the thrill of excitement coiled in her belly.

"Hi." Togi stretched her seatbelt over her ample chest and secured herself. "This is nice being able to drive over. It will give us a chance to get to know each other."

The sports car moved, growling like a big cat. The headlights bounced a shine off of the glass fronts of the humble shops that lined Main Street. Main Street was the only way to 70, and 70 was the only way to Idaho Springs.

"My goodness. We're so low to the ground," remarked Togi. "I feel like I could roll down the window and touch it."

"Used to trucks, right?" asked Maya with a smile.

There was dead silence. Maya checked her. Togi was staring.

"Did I say something wrong?" She turned to go to the main road that would take them to Idaho Springs.

"Well, yes." Her tight voice pinched off the words. "I'm used to trucks. I felt like that was a snub."

"For the record"—Maya tried to hold back her smile— "this is my late husband's car. I have only ever owned trucks. I was merely saying in a roundabout way I had the same experience."

"Ohh," said Togi before laughing. "I apologize. I didn't mean to be touchy. This will be perfect. We're going to do a lot of growing together."

"Is that what the kids are calling it these days?" she joked. "Growing? Let's just make an agreement that I'm not here to play or talk down to you and you aren't either. Because what you think I'm doing you're doing. You talk down to me because you think I'm rich. Let's just agree that we're two people with a common problem trying to get better."

"Okay. We might have to remind each other of that a couple of times, but I can accept that."

Once she wove through town, she put her foot to the floor and the Porsche flew to the Interstate 70 exit.

Togi braced herself. "Yeah, we're not in a hurry."

"Sorry." She braked. Maybe she was too excited.

"Are you trying to get away from Kevin?" Togi asked with a laugh. "I'm surprised we don't see him in the rearview mirror."

Maya flinched. *Had she just put Kevin down?*

"What? No. I like Kevin. A lot."

"You would be the first."

"What do you mean by that?" Maya prepared to defend him. "He's a great man."

"He was forever after that Lucy Shoemaker," said Togi. "Didn't she marry one of you all? A brother or a cousin?"

"You mean John's Lucy?" asked Maya with rising jealousy. "Kevin liked Lucy?"

It was the first she had heard of it, but then Kevin and she didn't talk about much personal stuff. It was all just day-to-day stuff—although he knew more about her personal history than the other way around. She wasn't so sure if she was comfortable knowing he did have a girlfriend or two, after all.

"Everybody in Blackwood liked Lucy. She was a popular kid coming up, but Kevin fell for her. Everyone in town knew it. Kevin's mom used to hit the sauce and Lucy's mother died so they were kind of buds for a while, but she outgrew him. It makes little sense that such a good looking guy like he is, a football star at one point, could be so silly shy."

"We're in a 12-step group, Togi. We really aren't ones to talk. We have quirks up the kazoo, and no offense, but this sounds like gossip. He's been an amazing support to me since I got here. He's never been untoward or tried to take advantage of me in any way. I consider him my best friend."

"You're absolutely right. I apologize."

"For real, please."

"I mean it," she said. "I apologize. You're not what I expected."

"How's that?"

"I didn't think you would be as respectable as you are."

"Because I'm rich?"

"Well, yeah," Togi answered honestly.

She wasn't sure now if Kevin hadn't been right. She was steamed with Togi's insinuation that Kevin was weird, but the rich thing got to her. One way or the other it was about her money unless it came down to Kevin.

"I got you mad, didn't I?"

"I'll get over it," she said evenly. "I'm not used to being out of my comfort zone. This is a good thing."

In no time, the women were coming up to Colorado Street to the United Church of Idaho Springs where the "big" meeting was. Even though Colorado Boulevard was fairly busy relative to the quieter side streets, she parked illegally on the street in front of the church.

"Ahem." Togi cleared her throat.

"Oh my gosh." Maya laughed. "I'm a serial illegal parker."

She started the car and parked in the parking lot with the rest of the meeting goers.

"I'm not sure what I have about following the rules," she confessed.

"Welcome to the club where we are more alike than different."

"Oh yeah?" she asked curiously. "What rule do you break?"

"We all have a thing to work on. You know what it is. I have to work on being less judgmental."

"This will be good," she noted again, in light of her honesty. "Let's enjoy our meeting."

"Yes, let's."

The mountain air was chilly and in contrast, the meeting room was nice and warm. Something about gathering in schools and churches created comfort. Technically they weren't comfortable places. The room was lined with rows of metal chairs and the floors were usually linoleum, but Maya found the spaces inviting.

Even outside of Blackwood, everyone knew Togi because she was what was known as an old timer. She had been sober for over thirty years straight. They knew Maya because she was an obvious Blackwood. Even if they weren't sure, with her signature height and dark hair and complexion, people pegged her for one eventually. The fact that at the end of her drinking career she had been a loud, obnoxious fixture in Idaho Springs in the not-too-distant past had also created a name for herself.

The two women sat next to each other after they got coffee. The awkwardness between them seemed to slip away. She got coffee because it was something to do. She only liked to drink it in the morning, but it gave her something to fidget with when she sat through the meetings.

She tended to check the door and people watch. Someone entered the room that jarred something in her. She knew she knew him, but she didn't know from where. Then it all came flooding back to her. It was the man she'd gotten busted with by her family when they hauled her to rehab. According to her brother Clem, he had been soaking her, convincing her to take money out of one of her accounts.

He was actually a superb-looking man, but all the pretty in the world couldn't mask the evil that was in his persona. They locked eyes for a moment. She couldn't remember his name, but she remembered the face. If she had been sober, there was no way she would have hooked up with him—if she did in fact "hook up." Obviously, he remembered her. He got his coffee and sat right next to her.

"Hey, Stretch," he said with mock affection.

He had a nickname for her. She turned to Togi, a little shaken.

"Can we move?"

Togi leaned forward and checked out the man next to her.

"Sure." She gave the man the eye.

Maya had obviously touched a nerve. He looked like he was amused, but he didn't appear to like her rejection of him.

"You know this is a mixed meeting," he said. "Maybe you'd be more comfortable at a women's meeting tomorrow night."

"I think I'm at my limit," she whispered so only Togi could hear. "This morning I was in the saloon. I knocked on the door at six in the morning just in case someone was there prepping for the day."

"That's important to know," said Togi.

"Yeah. I've been through a whole array of feelings today. I

went from feeling like I needed a drink, to being happy to see Kevin, to meeting you and all of that—"

"Quite a day for sure, but it evens out as you go on. Not so much wreckage of the past to contend with."

"I want to work the steps with someone and have a sponsor. I had one but she never picked up."

She realized she was risking feeling sorry for herself. The presence of the stranger slammed her with the shame for having one time sunk so low.

"You did call this morning before you went to the saloon. What's her name?" Togi's tone was serious.

"Cheryl Ann."

"Yeah, no." Togi shook her head. The strands of fire-red hair shifted but stayed pointed at the ceiling. "Honey, she's in rehab."

Maya's jaw dropped.

"For corn sake, no one told me," she said. "What I'm saying is, I don't think this is supposed to be a place where people judge or should feel threatened."

"I said if you are serious about this, I'll work with you. We just have to get to know each other." She nodded in the man's direction. "Who's that fella?"

"He's what I guess you could call a semi-blackout ghost. I was here in this town, ripping on a gambling tear with this guy when my brother and my cousins hauled me off to rehab."

"Focus on the positive. Just because people are sitting in these chairs doesn't mean we are perfect. We do our best and sometimes it takes a newcomer to call us on our bullshit, like you did me today. This guy won't be here much longer. Just wait."

She gave the guy a final glance. "Before I forget, I already emailed our family's attorney about the fact they fired you guys."

"You did?" Togi's eyes opened wide with genuine surprise.

"Yes. We had an agreement. I can't help but wonder if we didn't make an enormous mistake. The people we sold to don't seem to have their act together."

"Thank you. I appreciate that and we can talk about that another time. For now, let's focus on the here and now. Sit on the other side of me and let's have a good meeting. You earned your seat. No one can kick you out."

"Shh," the man from Maya's past scolded them.

"The meeting hasn't started yet," snapped Togi.

Maya giggled. She was right about Togi protecting her.

The meeting secretary approached Togi and said the person who was supposed to lead the meeting hadn't shown and asked if she could do it.

"How much time do you have to have?" asked Togi.

The secretary smiled because everyone there knew she had been sober a lot of years.

"Six months." He stared at her in disbelief. "I think you qualify, Togi. You've been sober longer than I've been alive."

Togi turned to Maya.

"Ever lead?" Togi asked with a smile.

"Are you being mean again?" Her stomach twisted with knots.

"I'm not." Togi laughed her head off. "I'm your friend. You can do it."

"I haven't prepared," she protested.

"Honey, you prepared by finding your way here."

CHAPTER SEVEN

Kevin

Kevin had planned to be in Idaho Springs at the tail end of the meeting, but he was so early that he had to wait from the beginning. When the smokers mashed their butts on the concrete and headed inside, the meeting would start, so he got out of his car and leaned on the building outside the door.

It was cold, and he remembered when Maya had been out earlier, she hadn't been wearing a coat or a sweater. He looked at his watch and figured he had time. One street over on Miner Street where all the shops were, he had a few minutes to pick her up something. He hopped back in the truck and hit a shop called Eldora's.

It was a posh boutique that was immensely popular. It was too impractical for his tastes, but he suddenly had the urge to splurge. He picked out a beautiful tailored buff-colored leather jacket he thought would be hot on her. It was his first present to her. If she was amenable, it would be the first of many.

Stills of every detail of Maya's form flowed through his mind as he estimated whether it would fit her. He recalled what it felt like to hold her and he had to put that from his mind while he was in public. She was a long-limbed, lean woman but her breasts were full. There was only one in the size he thought would work.

"I can bring this back if it doesn't fit, right?"

"Of course." The shop clerk rang it up and bagged it.

In a matter of minutes, he had a coat for Maya. He went back to the church where the meeting was held and waited outside. He had on his own leather jacket so he was comfortable in the crisp air.

He looked up to the horizon, to the mountains as he did so many times a day. Even though they were shadows in the darkness of the night, he still felt gratitude. He loved where he lived. He had no regrets about not staying a player when he had the chance. He loved his small-town life.

Kevin could hear the meeting clear as a bell. He was familiar with the general format. It was just getting through the business matters, so he had made it back from the store in plenty of time.

When they called the speaker for the evening, Maya B, he nearly choked. His heart brimmed with pride. He wanted to go in and listen, but that wouldn't be fair to her. He hadn't asked, and he hadn't told her he was coming. He might make her nervous. Plus, he wanted to keep his arrival a surprise.

Instead, he stayed outside with an ear to the door and listened. The words she spoke about being a shy, insecure kid stemming from being the tallest in class to the loss of her beloved husband touched him deeply. She was so eloquent and honest.

She talked about twenty minutes and then she opened the meeting up for others to share. Finally, some man spoke. Kevin was going to go back to his car but then he thought what the man was saying sounded awfully familiar—like he was sharing a story that Kevin had heard before, so he listened on. The man in the meeting was talking about Maya. He had to be. He mentioned an heiress whose family just sold a town. He was degrading her.

Kevin was going to step in the room, except that the guy finished his share, and it was the halfway mark of the meeting so they stopped for bathroom and coffee breaks, and to take up collections.

Maya stormed out of the meeting room with a man chasing after her and Togi trailing behind. They whizzed right by him because he wasn't standing in the light. Kevin didn't like what he saw. He recognized the signs of a hostile confrontation.

"Hey!" he yelled in a deep voice.

The guy trailing Maya didn't respond to his demand. In fact, he grabbed Maya's arm and yanked her back hard.

"You're coming with me," the man shouted. "You owe me for the last time."

Kevin charged from out of the shadows, with the Eldora's bag in hand. He moved across the parking lot in seconds and chest butted the guy. He knocked him flat, dropped the bag and bounded on top of him, pressing him into the concrete. He turned to see if Maya was okay. She was in one piece but holding her arm. She cried quietly. The sight of her sorrow sapped him of his strength and distracted him.

The guy beneath him grabbed his ear. Kevin shifted until the man's hand was flat against the street. He had him completely pinned. He took a deep breath, lifted just enough to flip him and kept him in a wrestling hold.

"Maya, get my cuffs from my truck. The key is in my pocket."

Maya had to reach intimately into the front pocket of his jeans to pluck the keys free.

"Aw man, you're a cop?" moaned the guy.

"Togi, call 911."

Maya returned with the cuffs.

He watched her shiver. "Maya, take the bag. It's yours."

She removed the jacket from the bag and smiled brightly as she held it up to herself.

"For me?"

"I knew you didn't wear a coat," he said with a mild scolding.

He was hot now from the physical commotion but he could see his breath. In the cold, clear night air, she slipped on the jacket he'd bought for her. It fit perfectly, like he knew it would.

"Thanks," she beamed.

"The cops are coming," reported Togi.

She checked out the bag that Maya's coat had come in.

"Wow." Togi's eyes took in the bag. "Nice. I wish someone had bought me something from Eldora's."

"Kevin bought it for me," she said, making a face of adoration.

"Can you get off of me?" the man beneath him shouted. "I will sue."

"I'm happy to face you in court." Kevin placed the cuffs on the man's wrists. He clicked them into place and rose to his feet, lifting the guy with ease.

"This is overkill, don't you think?" He squirmed and fought his confinement. "I just wanted to talk to her."

"By grabbing her arm?" There was no kindness or patience in his voice. He turned to Maya. "Are you okay?" Funny how he could flip the switch from cross to compassionate.

"I'm fine. How come you're here?" It seemed to take her a moment to catch on that he didn't belong there. "You came to give me a jacket?"

"No, I had something I wanted to tell you." Kevin rocked back on his feet the way a young boy would before he asked a girl on a date.

She looked between him and the man in cuffs. "What did you come all this way to say?"

He leaned forward and kissed her. He held the guy in one hand while he cradled her neck with the other and pulled her close to kiss him. It was a slow, sensual kiss.

"That," he said, with heavy-lidded eyes. "That was the most important part of the message."

Maya seemed to study him. He felt like he'd put everything on the line and he couldn't predict the way she would respond. Risk felt horrible, and those few seconds that she took to move were an eternity. Then she leaped forward and threw her arms around him and kissed him back.

"Hey," protested the cuffed man. "Knock it off."

Kevin swept his feet so he would settle down. It forced the man to rely on him for balance.

"Cool it," Kevin warned.

Very quickly the Idaho Springs police arrived. Kevin's substation in Blackwood was a branch of the bigger local station so those coming onto the scene were fellow cops.

"Kevin?" asked one cop as he approached the scene. "What happened?"

"Maya Blackwood was being aggressively pursued by this guy, who verbally threatened her before assaulting her."

"Assault?" the cuffed man protested. "Do you call grabbing her assault?"

The cop smiled. "That's actually the definition of assault. Unwanted contact, especially if followed by a threat. Did we all hear his admission?"

Everyone nodded.

"Are you hurt?" Kevin asked her tenderly as he cupped her cheek.

She revealed her arm, which had visible fingerprints. He turned from the guy for fear he would lose his cool. He did his best to contain his rage so he could care for his woman.

"I don't want to go get it checked out tonight. I'll go tomorrow if I have to. Right now, I want to go home."

"I'm the one who got tackled!" the man shouted.

"You didn't," the cop laughed.

Kevin nodded. Red blushed his cheeks. "Yeah, I did."

"You should have never quit." The cop leaned toward the cuffed guy. "You got tackled by a Denver Bronco. Bam Bam."

Kevin's face burned.

"Not to mention her boyfriend. Make sure you jot that down." He tugged at the cuffs. "I'm so suing all of you."

"Good," whispered Kevin in as scary a voice as he could. He stepped toward the man and watched him flinch.

"Get me out of here before he hurts me again," begged the cuffed man.

"Okay," said the cop with a big smile on his face.

The cuffed man was walked to the squad car and tucked into the back seat. The cop and Kevin shook hands.

"We can talk tomorrow," the officer told Maya. "I know you want to get home, but we do have to get a statement."

"Sorry, Togi."

"Why?" Her voice was matter-of-fact. "It's over. We're not likely to ever have that kind of excitement here again. It's done."

"You still want to be my sponsor?"

"Yes." She waved her hands around like she was swatting mosquitos. "You didn't cause this."

Kevin looked at Maya's arm and then deep into her eyes. "Can you drive?"

"Yes, but I'll have to take it slower."

"Oh, good." Togi bounced on her feet with excitement. "We might actually live until tomorrow." She looked back toward the door, where several people craned their necks to see what was going on. "I would ordinarily suggest we finish the meeting, but I think we'll just be a distraction."

"I'll see you at John's." He brushed Maya's lips with a soft kiss and completely ignored Togi's snarky reply.

"I look forward to it," Maya purred. She kissed him one more time before they parted ways.

CHAPTER EIGHT

Maya

Maya and Togi strapped in for the ride home. She had a gazillion things swirling through her mind as she put the key in the ignition. Togi touched her hand.

"Let's take a second," she counseled. "Were you telling the truth—are you okay to drive?"

Togi had a mother's voice that made her want to cry. Now that the whole thing was over, she was becoming emotional, but she sucked it up.

"Are you and Kevin a thing?" she asked. Her question had the tone of warning in it.

"We're about to be." A flush of warmth heated her insides. "I hope."

"Remember, you just got sober. You also got attacked in a meeting and kissed by a cop. On top of that, you asked me to be your sponsor. Let's get grounded. Maybe limit our changes to one or two a month, rather than per day."

"If you're asking me which changes to make and which changes to keep, I pick Kevin first. I'll pass on the attack."

Togi laughed deeply. There was a gravelly character to her voice that made Maya think she had been a smoker at one time. She didn't seem to be one now.

"You wouldn't be the first person who put a person in front of their recovery."

"Did you?"

"Oh, hell yes. I work in the diner. I get to lay eyes on every good-looking man who lives in Blackwood and then some that don't. I have worked there for half my life. Honey, I fell in love a lot. As long as you don't pick up drinking again over it, you'll live. From now on let's take it one thing at a time. Are you well enough to drive? Did this guy hurt your arm?"

"Yes, and yes. It hurts, but it's not broken or anything."

"Okay then, while you drive, tell me the story about the guy they just hauled away. Any idea why he might think you owe him?"

"No." She turned the key and her car purred to life. "When I gambled, people pegged me for a Blackwood and they swarmed around me like bees to a hive."

"Because you have money?"

"Yes." She backed out of the spot and turned toward Blackwood. "I am fortunate, but I have to tell you, it brings out the crazies."

"Get a strong foundation under your feet, you won't have to worry about a thing."

"I'll try, Togi."

"Hopefully, this will make a colorful story to tell everyone when you become a speaker on the circuit. You sounded like a natural in there." Togi reached over and touched her arm warmly. "It's important to give back. There's a person out there waiting to find recovery. Kind of nice if you made sure you were ready to help when he or she arrives."

Even though she could not wait to be back in Blackwood and the evening had been dramatic, it hadn't been a total disaster. She'd found a friend in Togi. As she drove down Interstate 70 toward Blackwood, her head filled with thoughts of Kevin. He was a lot more pleasant to ruminate about than the drama she was driving away from. The image of him running to rescue her was seared into her brain. He was like a bull and he used his body so smoothly as a weapon. What he must have looked like on the field. She was consumed by him.

She must have been on automatic pilot because suddenly she was pulling up in front of Togi's house. Letting her go felt like she was breaking up with her.

"Thanks for going with me." She laid her hand gently on Togi's arm. "I think you and I are going to work well together. I don't know how you did it, but despite all that happened, I still wanna come back, and I want to give back."

Togi smiled a rare smile.

It warmed Maya's heart.

"Just wreckage from the past. Not your fault."

The once crusty waitress had transformed into a spiritual mentor and Maya considered herself fortunate.

"You know, at some point today I asked for direction and I got it. Thanks for taking me up on my request."

"Even if it was a half-assed joke?" grinned Togi.

"Yeah, even if."

She waited for her to leave her car and make it safely into her house. It was all she could do to hold off from calling Kevin. She pulled forward just enough so she rolled into the shadows. She took her phone out and dialed his number. She felt like she was sneaking a drink. Only she knew he wasn't a shot of whiskey or a glass of wine. He was a straight-up moonshine kind of a man and that might be more addictive than the booze.

"Hi," she whispered.

"Where are you and why are you whispering?"

"I just dropped Togi off. I'm in my car and about to head back to my house, I mean unless—"

She didn't want to go back to her house. It had been a long day and she still needed more of him.

"I know it's kind of late—" He paused as if he was considering her words carefully. "Do you think we can talk?"

"Sure." Her heart rate ramped up to a frenzied pace. The pounding in her chest made it hard to breathe. "Wanna meet at the saloon?"

"Do you think that's a good idea? Kind of the way we began our day."

"I'm fine, Kevin. It's not like there isn't alcohol everywhere you go and some places where you don't expect it. The saloon is open and it's close."

"Why not John's house?"

"Because it's twenty minutes away and Clem is there," she argued. "Why not your place?"

The truth was she was impatient to see him.

Kevin laughed.

She loved his laugh, but he was avoiding something again. She felt it in her bones.

"Clem being there is probably a good thing."

She got his meaning. They would be all over each other if they had the opportunity to be alone. Though they'd known each other for a while, it was all new and rushing things wouldn't be wise.

"We should talk, but what I have to say is personal, and I'm not sure I want to have the conversation in a saloon."

"I would have you over to my house, but I'm a bachelor and would rather get it ready for a guest."

"A guest?" She questioned. "Who are you calling a guest? I've never been to your place. That's silly to think I'd judge you by the tidiness of your living room."

"You're right but still ..."

"Okay." She let out an exasperated exhale. "John's house then. See you in a few." She looked down at her phone and pressed the red dot to end the call. *What am I going to do about Kevin?*

Once again, she headed through the nearly empty town on the route back to her cousin's house. The more she left Blackwood, the more she hated to leave. She thought more and more that maybe she and her family had sold the town in haste. They'd missed the important step of checking it out first. She wished that it had always been her home. Maybe the decision to sell wouldn't have been so easy to make.

She turned onto the private road and wound her way to John's house. Each time she pulled into the garage it felt less like home to her. It was a beautiful house, especially at night. Its immense pitched roof gave it the appearance of a ski chalet. It had the feel and look of a getaway. Its lighting had a magical hue, but it lacked something, mostly furniture. What there was, though, was at least comfortable.

The couch in the living room was super sumptuous and almost the width of a twin bed, but that was about all there was there. The bed in the room she'd chosen for herself was also nice. It happened to be the same bed that Kevin slept in when he first stayed there, a fact which had crossed her mind when she lay awake in it. Now that he had kissed her, it would be a different experience.

Otherwise, being at John's felt like she was just staying there temporarily. He had said she could do whatever she wanted to it but she'd done nothing. It wasn't her house. Maybe she didn't like it because it had been a bachelor pad, or maybe John didn't have a designer's touch. Her lack of excitement about the house could have been a thousand things, but she knew without a doubt that her dislike of the place was because it had no heart.

Those were the thoughts that ran through her mind from the car to the door. It was just evidence to her that she was ready to transition into her own life. That was the theme of the day.

She let herself in through the garage. She could see Clem's light spilling out from under the door. Though he might be awake, Kevin and she would have privacy in the living room. Kevin would show up in a few minutes, but it would feel like forever.

Finally, there was a tap on the door. Maya had kicked off her shoes and let the plush feel of the carpet soothe her soles as she made her way to greet him.

His expression was serious. He didn't rush to kiss her as she'd hoped he would. She was so eager to feel his lips on hers, but she followed his lead. He stepped forward and kissed her on the forehead, and then he kissed her on the bridge of the nose and then her lips.

It was a soft, sensual kiss, but after a moment, he withdrew from her like he was putting the brakes on. She couldn't believe how vulnerable she was all of a sudden. Her emotions were coiled into a tangled mess.

He took her by the hand and led her to the living room.

She was a grown woman, but she felt like a schoolgirl holding hands with her guy. They sat down, still apart like friends but a lot touchier. He didn't let go of her. He was trembling, which was so not like him. He always seemed so unflappable.

"I like you a lot," he began, his voice shaky.

She believed his confession to be true. She wanted to rush in and reply but she bit her lip and listened.

"But you're making a lot of changes in your life, and they're important ones." His soft look caressed her face. "I don't want to be a reason you don't do well."

Maya tilted her head, taking in his words. Words similar to Togi's. Cautionary words she didn't want to hear.

"I don't plan on going back to where I was when I came here. I never had a problem before my husband died."

"I know, sweetheart." He reached out and stroked her face. "But—"

"I'm good, Kevin." Her voice held conviction. "You don't have to worry about it."

He took her arm that the guy at the meeting hurt.

"How's this doing?"

"It's sore." Suspicious he had just changed the subject, she narrowed her eyes at him.

"We can go to Idaho Springs Hospital tonight or tomorrow," he said. "My mom works there."

"Not tonight." She looked down at the skin that was already bruising. "Are you okay with me meeting your mother? I mean, especially under these circumstances?"

"Yes. I'm okay with a lot of things. It's taking everything

for me to not act on impulse right now. I want to do this right."

"What are you saying?" Her insides were melting with the heat of desire. "Do you want to come upstairs?"

"I would love to." He kissed her in between each word. "But I have to do this right. We've waited this long to act on our attraction, or at least I've waited this long to tell you how I feel. I can wait longer."

"How long?" she asked, tensed with impatience. "When did you know you liked me, because I have been crushing on you for a long time?"

He smiled and kissed her again.

"I better stop doing that or I'll change my mind. How about you come over to my house and let me cook you dinner."

"I get to come over and see the bachelor pad?"

"You do if that's what you want. There's no rush."

"Are you a good cook?" She smiled after finding one more thing about him that was utterly attractive.

"Don't you remember?" he asked. "I cooked for you while I was here."

She made a face like that was a blur because it was. She was still missing chunks of time from her life.

"Okay, so that's the plan? You're going to make dinner for me?"

"Yes." His smile warmed her through and through. "I have stuff to tell you I didn't before."

Her chest tightened with fear. Was he going to answer the

question about why he was unattached and why he'd waited so long to make a move? Was this where he told her she wasn't exactly his type?

"Maya." He took her hand in his. "My mom is in recovery too."

"Yes, Togi mentioned that today." She let out a laugh.

It wasn't the right response to such a heartfelt disclosure but she was so relieved that what he said wasn't a big deal.

"I meant thank you for telling me." She held his hand tighter, hoping he wouldn't let go. "Now I get why you're so good with me."

He seemed bothered. "So Togi talked about me?" He arched his brow.

"All good," she assured him.

He pinched his lips together and shook his head. "So yes, my mom was or is an alcoholic. When I was young and because she was sick as we used to call it, and my father never wanted to be at home to deal with her, I was in charge."

She reluctantly let go of his hand and cupped his cheek. "That was awful, I'm sure. You were just a child."

Her parents weren't home much, but at least they'd had nannies and never had to do much for themselves.

"Is that how you learned to be a great cook?" she asked.

"Yep."

"Kevin, I think it's high time someone cooked for you."

"I'd like that." He leaned into her touch. "How about I go

first, and then you take as many turns after that as you want?"

He lowered his head and kissed her. Those few sentences told her so much. They explained why he was so careful. He had a lifetime of missteps. He didn't want to invite trouble into his world. A flood of realization poured into her consciousness as she got it on so many levels.

She wrapped her arms around his massive body and held on. His hands roamed her back until they cradled her. His wet, warm tongue swept inside her mouth and she was in heaven. Then his forearm grazed her arm and she winced.

"That bad, huh?"

His voice was never truly angry sounding when he was mad, so it was hard to tell what he felt now, but she was getting more attuned to him and she knew he was upset because her arm was injured. He walked them into the kitchen where the light was brightest. He looked at her bruised spot and felt it gently.

"I don't think it's broken."

"I don't think he could break it by just grabbing me."

"He could," Kevin spoke with authority. "Someone rushes you with force and just the right angle and you end up with fractures. I didn't push you to go to the ER right away but I should have. It's easy for people when they're injured to dismiss it but take this seriously."

"On the other hand, I think he might have to get a few x-rays," she chuckled. "Good Lord. You were like a locomotive.

I wished I'd seen you in action back in the day." She replayed the tackling scene once again in her memory.

"It was kind of fun."

"You will probably get sued."

"Yeah, probably," he said with a nod and a grin.

"You don't care?"

"Not a bit."

CHAPTER NINE

Kevin

Hard as it was for him to wait, Kevin decided he and Maya would have dinner on the evening of his next day off, which was two days away. On the first of those two days, he started off his morning as he always had, driving through the streets, checking on everyone. Only this morning, he was ridiculously tired because he had lain awake with thoughts of Maya so vivid that it was as if they'd spent the entire night together.

He checked in with Damon at the saloon before heading to the diner for a cup of coffee. Many of the people who lived in Blackwood were blue collar and they rose early. Being there when they rolled in for breakfast was a great way for Kevin to connect.

There were a number of customers at the diner counter. There was a lone man sitting in a big booth, staring out the window where pitch black veiled the Rocky Mountains. He appeared to be perpetually asking the question "Why?"

The man was Samuel Clemens Blackwood named after the novelist. *Clem* as he was called, was Maya's brother. Kevin slipped onto the bench in front of him. The man looked so distraught.

"Hey." He knew he interrupted the view and his presence would force Clem to engage.

"You're up early."

Clem laughed sarcastically and nodded.

"Your detective skills are good," Clem said acidly.

He shook his head and laughed. He vividly recalled how snarky Maya had been those first few days when she'd moved here fresh out of rehab. She was a biter.

"What's going through your mind?" He leaned back, making himself comfortable.

"I don't understand," whispered Clem, picking up his thoughts midway through. "I gave her everything. I don't get why she needed something more or why she couldn't just stay home while she had more."

Clem looked haggard with his wrinkled clothes, unkempt hair, and withering physique. He didn't look like he'd eaten in a while. Kevin casually poked his finger in the air to signal the early morning waitress. She was at their table fast.

"Can I get a side of fries and two waters, please?" he asked, speaking quietly so he didn't disturb Clem's thought process.

"If you want to talk about it, I'm a good listener. That's

the great thing about being a cop in a small town like this. No crime. I have nothing but time. Or not. Whatever."

"Met her in school." Clem cracked and he swallowed hard. "We were Deadheads together. Now I can't listen to 'Touch of Grey' without wanting to sob like a child."

The waitress sat two short glasses of iced water and the fries on the table top and left.

Kevin moved the fries in between them. He set the ketchup and the salt and pepper by the plate. He hoped the sight and smell of the fries would entice Clem to eat something.

Other than that, he said nothing—didn't push. He let the man have his space to release a little bit before he changed the subject so he wouldn't be so self-focused.

"Your sister's doing well." He made small talk, hoping Clem would engage.

Clem lifted his head but didn't look Kevin in the eye.

"Yeah? Didn't know how that one would go, right?"

"Right." He let the parallel find its way into Clem's mind. He just wanted to plant the seed of comparison. If Maya's life could turn around, so could his.

"I think she's learning the trick to finding something to be grateful for even in trying times. Did she tell you what happened at the meeting last night?" He reached for the ketchup and squeezed a puddle on the side of the plate.

"No." Clem picked up a fry. He salted it and dunked it into ketchup.

Kevin was happy to see the man eat.

"There was a guy there—the same one she was with when you took her to rehab. He was at the meeting. He grabbed her." He redirected Clem's focus from his sorrows to Maya. It seemed to work.

"Jeez, Louise." Clem lifted his head and straightened up. "That guy is trouble."

"Appears to be. You don't happen to know his name, do you? He's in the Idaho Springs Jail so if you don't remember, I can check in with them."

"No, I can't remember. I know he had gotten his hooks into her fast and she was so out of it, she didn't even know."

"Looks like it's time he paid the price for messing with her." Kevin wished he'd tackled the man harder. Maya had left with an injured arm where her assailant had only injured his ego, if that. "Maya held her own."

"Man," Clem remarked. "I'm proud of her. She's come a long way. I remember those first few days in rehab we were so afraid she would sign herself out."

"I'll bet you she never thought she'd be where she is today."

"You like her, don't you?" Clem asked.

"Yes." There was no doubt in his mind. Like seemed like such an inadequate word for his feelings for Maya.

"Does she know? Because we've talked about you and it sounds like both of you are keeping secrets from one another." Clem grabbed another fry. "Take it from me, secrets are like a flesh-eating bacterium to relationships." He sipped his water and snatched another fry and then another and another. It took time but eventually, half the plate was gone.

He noted Clem put salt and hot sauce on his fries, which meant Kevin wasn't having any. That made him laugh softly.

"Is that what happened to you? Secrets?"

Clem shook his head. "I can't even think about my own situation right now. My brain hurts from too much thought; it's wearing me thin."

"Looks like it. Hate to say it, but you look like hell." He generally kept his opinions to himself but this was Maya's brother and if anything happened to him, it would stall Maya's progress. "Did you drive here?"

"I rode my bike," confessed Clem.

He tried not to show his alarm, but Clem was smart enough to know Kevin knew riding a bike in the dark on a winding mountain road was suicidal.

"I was going to ask you to ride around with me in the patrol car. It's not fast paced, but it's fun."

Clem considered his request for a moment. "I'd like that."

"I would enjoy the company. Let's get a couple coffees to go. I can take you home later. We can put your bike in the substation for now. It'll be safe." He would conveniently not be available to return it until he was sure Clem was stable. "Finish those." He gently nudged the fries toward him.

"You didn't have any."

"I'm waiting to have breakfast with your sister. You eat."

"Actually, now I'm starved." Clem gobbled down the fries.

"Have some bacon and eggs. You've got a pool of hot sauce to use."

"Do we have time?" Clem looked outside at the sky, which was just showing a hint of blue. "I would like to roll with you."

"I rarely allow it, but if you want to get that order to go, I'll let you eat in the cruiser."

Clem ordered the bacon and eggs along with another side of fries to be rolled up in a large flour tortilla. He put packets of salt and pepper in his pockets and ordered a large coffee to go while Kevin watched in fascination. When he finished, he followed him to the car.

He was happy he had someone to ride with. His job was solitary in nature so this would be nice.

Clem's bike sat out front. He went back inside to get the busboy, who he offered twenty bucks to take it over to the station, but Clem bumped it up to a hundred.

"Jeez." He shook his head at Clem's generosity.

"I have the money," said Clem quietly. "I like to share it. If I'm asking someone to help me because I don't have my shit together, he should be compensated well."

"Not bad compensation for ten minutes' worth of work," Kevin observed with a smile.

The bus boy took the bike and fist bumped the air several times as he crossed the street.

"Looks like I made his day."

"Kindness is always an effective balm for what ails you," he replied.

The sun was cracking the sky as the two men loaded into the cruiser and pulled out of the diner parking lot. He had just patrolled all of Blackwood not an hour before, but he repeated it for Clem's sake.

Something told him he would get a call or a text from Maya. The feeling pressed on his midsection and nagged at him. He had been right, she'd called, but he knew she would. He had learned to trust his intuition over the years.

"Morning." She was on the speakerphone.

"Good morning, sexy." The purr of her voice shot bolts of desire through his body.

"Oops." He shifted in his seat. "I have your brother in the car. You're on speakerphone."

Clem burst out laughing. He laughed so hard he nearly dropped his coffee and burrito.

"What's going on?" Maya asked with concern in her voice.

"Nothing. Just hanging out with your brother."

"Why is Clem in the car?"

"We're bonding," He said like it was the most natural thing in the world.

"Are we still having dinner tonight?"

"No, we're having dinner on Friday."

"I may be jealous of Clem. He's getting time with you that I want."

"I'm going to patrol with your brother and then I'll swing by so you don't have to be jealous." He made a kissing sound into the phone before he hung up.

"You and my sister, man." Clem shook his head and smiled. "That makes me happy."

"Thanks." Kevin smiled. "Makes me happy too."

The sky was purple and gold and orange and the sun rose like a shiny golden coin into the sky. The colors splashed against the Rockies.

"That sunrise is a masterpiece." Clem leaned forward and stared out the window as they made their way down Main Street.

"Pretty, right?"

"Never gets old," Clem said with a fading voice. "We should have never sold this place. I feel like a jackass because now I want to come home."

CHAPTER TEN

Maya

It was early but Maya wanted to get to work on the matter of the town's buyers backtracking on promises. She showered and threw on a simple outfit of skinny jeans—which for her were any pair she owned—and a loose sweater. She knotted her long, dark hair and got busy.

She drafted an email and then proofed it. It was pretty good, if she said so herself. She sent it to Blackwood Corporation's counsel, who happened be her cousin-in-law, Deena, Caleb's new wife. She wanted to alert Deena about what the people in town were saying and offer a draft response.

"Thank you, counselor," Deena replied quickly.

Maya smiled. For a moment she wondered if she might like to be a lawyer. She padded to the kitchen in slippers to boil water for peppermint tea.

Kevin's cruiser pulled up. She leaned on the cabinet and

peeked out the curtain of the side window and just spied on him.

She adored how Clem and he looked like they were getting on well. Clem's face was actually bright and the dark circles were at least not so stark. However, he shuffled into the house like he was exhausted.

"Dead man walking," laughed Clem.

"That's funny," she said. "Not."

Kevin leaned in and kissed her. It was novel and refreshing that he could do that.

"How'd you get into town?" She looked out the window to the opened garage. "I see your car is still here."

"Bike."

Her face dropped. "Are you serious?" she asked, yelling at him. She was livid to the point of tears. She shoved Clem and the smiles left everyone's faces.

"Wow." Kevin moved forward and grabbed her hands. "No hitting." His tone was serious. "I don't care if he is your brother."

She felt so helpless that all she could do was weep. She knew what Clem was doing. She'd been there herself, though she wasn't aware of it at the time. Clem didn't have the excuse of being numbed with alcohol. "You could have been killed."

Clem stooped so that they were face to face. "But I wasn't," he replied. "And I don't want to be and that's the most important part."

"I know it's not about me, but I just lost someone. I can't live through that again," she pled.

"You won't have to. I want to find the happiness you have. Now, if you'll excuse me, I have to get some sleep because I'm so damn tired." He shook Kevin's hand. "Thanks, man. I appreciate everything you did." Clem walked past them and upstairs.

Kevin gazed at Maya.

"What happened?" she asked him.

He pulled her head close to his lips and whispered, "I'll tell you in a sec, but not so that I break his confidence. I can answer some things, but he confided in me. I can't break that trust."

"Tell me what you can."

"He was out at five in the morning, and I was there. We just hung out and he feels better. You'll have to talk to him yourself, but I think he will be okay."

She threw her arms around him and kissed him with everything she had.

"Thank you." She nuzzled her face into his neck and breathed in the calming scent of him. "I'm so mad at Kaitlin for breaking his heart."

"I think he just learned, through your strong example, that he will be fine." He brushed his lips against hers. "Eventually he'll be able to move on and it won't hurt so much."

"I'm almost glad I had to go to rehab."

"You get to be his shining light." Kevin grinned. "Now you don't have to be ashamed of your past."

"Or shut the door on it. You were his shining light this morning." Maya knew she was falling deeper and deeper in love with him. "And mine."

"Let's take you over to Idaho Springs Hospital and get your arm checked out."

"I think I'm fine." She touched her arm and tried not to wince.

"I have motives for doing this. One, I think this guy will come back at you or me or both and we need a record."

"Check," she said. "That's smart thinking from a smart cop. I'm on board with that."

"And two, my mom is there. She works the help desk."

"Aw." she was touched. "I should go clean up then."

"You look fine." He shook his head as if to erase the words. "You look more than fine. You do nice things to jeans."

A red-hot rush colored her face in the places where the tears had wet her skin.

"Oh, my gosh I love that you told me you like me. I like to get compliments," she gushed.

She kissed him slowly. Tendrils of electricity unfurled and arced through her body.

Kevin was definitely responding, their bodies slowly dancing.

"Let's go," he whispered drowsily.

"Upstairs?" Her voice was soft and seductive.

"No, to the hospital," he replied. "I'm about to cave."

"Really?" she asked hopefully.

He arched his brow and she backed off.

He wanted to do things the way he wanted to do them and, in this case, she let him have his way, but she would work on his spontaneity.

She gathered her purse and followed him to the cruiser. It never occurred to her that it might be scandalous for her to be riding shotgun in a police car until they got out on the highway and other drivers checked her out.

"You know—" Nerves made her voice tremble. "I'm not sure it's the best way to meet your mom. Because of the drama and stuff. I'm embarrassed. I got a sober reminder of how bad it was for me. That guy was awful. I must have been in a horrible place. I didn't think I was *that* bad, but I guess I was."

"Maya," he replied. "She works in a hospital. She sees drama every day, and like I said, she was in your shoes at one time. Besides, we've talked about you, and she wants to meet you."

"You did?" She perked up. "She does?"

Idaho Springs Hospital was twenty minutes away from John's house which was another twenty minutes away from the town of Blackwood, creating a perfect triangle between the three points.

Even in the still cool weather of the early spring, there were signs of life in the foliage along the highway where there weren't jagged stone fronts erupting from the earth. Spring was the season for rebirth. What a perfect time to start something with someone as wonderful as Kevin. He parked in the area reserved for law enforcement and Maya smiled.

"You pretty much always have a parking spot, don't you?"

He smiled a slow but bright smile. "I do. It's one of the perks."

He got her door for her. He was such a gentleman—a big, gorgeous well mannered man. She was jittery and nervous to meet his mother.

"I'm kind of scared."

"No need to be." He rested his hand at the small of her back. "If it makes you feel better, she's probably nervous too. It's best to jump in with both feet."

Maya laughed. "That is so silly coming from you, the man who refused to jump at all until yesterday." She wrapped her arm around his waist and leaned into him. "I respect that you want to keep it on the down low." She walked forward. "Let's go."

He knew exactly what she was talking about and stopped. He swept his hands up to cup her face and kissed her as if to prove her wrong.

"I'm not keeping anything on the down low. I'm just moving slowly. I want to do it right, but mark my words, it'll be wherever and whenever after that. Got it?"

Maya thought she was going to faint. She was so over-loaded thinking about the possibilities that she couldn't bother being nervous meeting his mother. Her biggest fear now was of his mother knowing why she was so flushed and how her son made Maya pulse with need.

They walked inside the hospital. It smelled of antiseptic and flowers.

The help desk was in the lobby's center. A tiny, brown-haired woman manned the desk. Maya always thought those desks looked rather futuristic, like they belonged in a spaceship.

"That's your mom?"

"Yep. Her name is Franny. Franny Hoisington."

She took in the tiny woman. "But you're so big and fair and she's tiny and dark-haired."

"I look like my dad. Mom's hair was a lighter brown like mine when she was younger." He threaded his fingers through hers and gave her a squeeze.

They had to stop whispering because there were only so many steps from the entrance of the door to Franny's desk.

She looked up from her work and smiled at the sight of Maya and Kevin.

"Hello," she greeted them with definite excitement in her voice.

"Mom." Kevin smiled like a kid on Christmas morning. "This is Maya Blackwood. Maya, this is my mother, Franny Hoisington."

"Just call me Franny." She grinned from ear to ear. "My goodness. Nice to meet you."

How Franny smiled so intensely and talked at the same time, Maya didn't know, but she decided Kevin's mother was adorable. Both Maya and Kevin towered over her as she came around the desk to give Maya a hug. It was hard to believe the giant man standing next to her was related to the tiny woman embracing her.

He interrupted the hug fest. "Mom, we're here to say hi and to get Maya's arm checked out."

"Oh, okay."

Maya noted the absence of any intrusive questions about what was wrong with her arm. She thought that was considerate.

"ER is that way." She pointed to the left hallway marked as the emergency room. "The triage nurse will process you in." She gave them both another squeeze. "Have a nice day and nice to meet you, dear."

"Nice to meet you too."

She waited until they were through a set of double doors until she made a remark.

"I think I can still feel your mother smiling."

"Yep," Kevin said with a mild smile on his own face. "Meeting you made her happy. She's happiest when I'm happy, and you make me happy." He led her down the corridor. "Has anyone from the Idaho Springs Police Department contacted you about last night? They can only hold him overnight unless you press charges. Do you want to press assault charges?"

"I don't think so." She nibbled on her lower lip, thinking about the consequences of both pressing charges and not. "I should, I guess, but I want to put it behind me."

That was what she thought she would do, but when the intake nurse learned that her bruised arm happened during an assault, she informed Maya that the hospital had to file a police report.

"I get it." Sadness seeped into her soul.

"It's nothing to be upset about," said the nurse.

"I just don't want to deal with it. I'm ready to move on."

She turned to Kevin. "Did you set me up here?" She wasn't upset one way or the other, she just wanted to know.

"In the back of my mind I knew the procedure, but no, I only wanted to have it looked at. The way it happened, you can get what they call a greenstick fracture." He looked down at his body. "I know all about walking around with fractures and not even knowing it."

Once she was x-rayed, they had to wait for the radiologist to read the results.

"You broke a bone." The doctor looked intently at the films.

"I did?" Maya leaned forward to look at the x-rays clipped to the light-box.

"I'm sorry," he corrected himself. "I mean you have before."

He drew his finger along some area that made no sense to Maya.

"I've never broken a bone," Maya responded.

"This is fairly recent. Within the last year or so, but there aren't any new breaks. You have a pretty good bruise, which I guess you know. The nursing staff will send some home care instructions. All it needs is ice and time."

She was grateful she had no severe injuries because as

time wore on, her arm hurt more and more. She couldn't shake the shock of having broken her arm and not knowing it. It was a bitter pill to swallow. Just showed how bad things had been for her.

"What?" asked Kevin.

"I keep getting these reminders of how awful my life was." She hated the time she'd lost over the last year. Hated how avoiding her grief only created more. "I'm shocked."

The whole process reminded her of where her drinking had taken her in such a short period of time, and how she'd become such a bad person. If anything good came out of it, it had to be that her drunkenness had brought her Kevin.

CHAPTER ELEVEN

Kevin

If Maya thought she was nervous meeting his mother. He was nervous knowing what the evening would bring. Whether he gave in to spontaneity or planned everything so it was just right, he knew he would have a certain amount of performance anxiety.

He'd planned a dinner for them, steak, salad, French bread and instead of wine, he got Italian sparkling soda flavored with orange. He'd prepped everything the night before and planned to cook after Maya arrived.

Instead of picking her up and bringing her over as he ordinarily would, she opted to drive. That gave him more time. He worked painstakingly over every detail, making sure everything about their first real date was just right.

He heard the purr of the Porsche pull into his driveway.

He spied on her. Watching her as she exited. He salivated

over the way she moved, the way her hair bounced as she strutted from her car to the door. She strutted and had every reason to. She looked smoking hot in a leather skirt and flimsy white blouse. Maya didn't need to wear super short skirts because she was so tall. Miles of legs he wanted wrapped around his waist peeked from beneath the material. He ached from the inside out for this woman.

He glanced down at his own clothes and wondered if he should have changed again. This was the third outfit he'd put on in the last hour. Wearing a black polo shirt and khakis, he hoped he wasn't underdressed.

He opened the door and tried his best not to maul her, but his need for her took on a life of its own. It went beyond the physical. He was certain his feelings had gone past lust to love. For ten months, he'd been holding back and hiding his passion. It was nice to be in love with someone and have them return the feelings.

"Beautiful." Seeing her sucked the oxygen right out of the air. "You're absolutely beautiful."

She beamed as bright as the sun under his compliment.

"While we're dishing compliments"—a pink blush colored her cheeks—"you're so handsome." Her eyes sparkled with passion. "I don't know if I've told you that before, but you are so damn good looking." She closed her eyes and bit her lip in the most seductive of ways. "I can't get the image of you running to my rescue out of my mind. I wish I'd seen you play football."

"I do have clips," he said self-consciously. "We can watch

them together, but showing you the NFL clips isn't a move to influence or attract you. It's a way to share my life with you."

Maya giggled and he thought he would die and ascend to heaven. He loved her laugh.

"You asserted your influence and made your move when you had a bad guy in hand."

She lifted her face to kiss him.

"Hold on, I have to turn off the stove," he whispered.

"Why?" Her voice was as whisper soft as his.

"Because I am not waiting till after dinner." He pulled her close. "Can you stay the weekend with me? I feel this might take a while."

"Yeah," she purred. "One perk of being blissfully unemployed and hot for you is I'm available."

"Not anymore you're not."

Racing into the kitchen, he turn off the oven. When he returned, he swept Maya into his arms and moved down the hallway. One soft kick opened the bedroom door so he could carry her inside. Filled with need and desire, he wanted to rush, but had to slow it down in order to think straight. Could a mind be too jumbled to know what to do next?

He lay with her on the bed stroking her hair, admiring her beautiful face and staring into her eyes. He brushed her lips with a whisper-light touch and closed his eyes to savor the wonder of contact with her.

He kissed her cheeks and the bridge of her nose, trailing

his lips to her jawline just below her ear until she shivered. The sensitive spot needed to be explored more.

Kevin tortured Maya, brushing his lips over that tender nook until she writhed and moaned. He quickly found her erogenous zones and learned that the curve of her neck made her react passionately. Maya clutched at his hair, holding on for dear life or holding him in place because she feared he might leave. He would never leave.

He trailed his mouth down her arm, kissing the soft inside of her elbow, all the way down to her hand. He traced the inside of her wrist with the tip of his tongue.

Feeling emboldened, he unbuttoned her blouse, slowly and methodically. His mind was screaming to tear it free, but he took his time. They say your first is by far the best and this was his first time making love to anyone. He'd had plenty of sex, but never with someone he loved.

Her blouse fell open, giving him free access to the swell of her breasts.

Maya wore a lavender satin push-up bra that was so beautiful against her tawny skin. Though long and lean, she was also full-breasted with curves. Curves that fit perfectly in his palms.

How many times had his eyes dropped and fixed on her beauty and his heart wished she was in his arms? At long last, he was touching her and he couldn't believe it.

He unfastened the front clasp and let the fabric fall free. Her beautiful breasts spilled into his hands. He lowered his mouth to pull her nipple between his lips. He wanted to be gentle, not rush in, but he couldn't help himself. His heart beat for her. His body trembled thinking about what would come next. He refocused his attention when Maya's hands worked the buttons of his pants.

He lifted and looked down. They worked together to shed their clothes until they were body to body. Kevin could not get over the unbelievable softness of her skin. Her silky thighs glided up his and soon he was nestled in between them.

This moment was long overdue in many respects, but he didn't want to hurry through their first time. There was so much to savor that he had to make it last. He kissed her, sweeping her hair up with his hands as his tongue moved inside her sweet mouth.

Maya took his hand and placed it between them. She was slick and hot.

"You do that to me." Her words were breathy and so damn sexy.

He held her hand against his aching hardness. "You do this to me."

Maya lifted her hips, reaching for his length. She wanted to hustle things along, and he wanted to slow it down. Surely, they could find a compromise, but first, he wanted them to know each other physically.

He trailed his lips down her middle, between her spectacular breasts, down the valley that lay softly between, along the line that traversed her incredibly flat stomach and further still. Maya's long legs bent and he settled in between, his shoulders now draped with those wondrous limbs as he kissed her in a new place.

Her moans filled the air. This would have been missed if they'd given in and made love in John's house with Clem there. Something about her expressing her passion in his bedroom made his house a real home. He'd been too long without a woman's comfort. Maya Blackwood was worth the wait.

He penetrated her with the length of his tongue, exploring and tasting and learning.

Her long fingers raked through his hair and stroked his face. When he looked up to check on her, an expression of ecstasy stared back at him.

Maya was easy to please and so responsive. Kevin sensed the signs of imminent pleasure approaching.

She tensed against his tongue, building up for release. He pressed against her most sensitive spot until she pulsed against his lips. The last shudder left her body before he rose above her. How he wanted to move from one moment seamlessly into the next, but he had no intention of letting her come down from the high of a climax. Reaching for a condom, he fumbled getting it open due to his hands shaking with so much need and nervousness.

Impatient to move things along, Maya took the condom and tore the package carefully.

He watched as she rolled it down his length. Kevin thought he would lose it having her fingers touch him so intimately. He levered himself against the opening of her body and pressed inside then set up a slow rhythm—a relaxed pace that gave them time to explore their passion for each other.

The long, languid strokes would surely torture them both. It was more sweetness than either could stand.

Her hands explored his chest then moved to his back and settled on the globes of his ass to pull him deeper inside. This experience was more than he could imagine. More than he could have wished for. He wouldn't last. Couldn't last. But they had time to do it again and again. There was no better way to spend the night than making love to Maya.

Kevin nestled his face in the base of her neck where it flowed into her shoulder. He let go, allowing himself to find his pleasure—more pleasure than he'd ever known. Of all the good moments in his life, this was now the best. He knew without a doubt that he was completely in love with her.

She clutched him, her body tightening until a groan burst forth. She hung onto him as they rode their rapture out together. Their bond was created. Their eyes connected and he held her gaze through smoky, heavy lids.

With a touch to his cheek, Maya regarded him with such affection as their pleasure peaked and ebbed.

Finally, after the last shudder subsided, they crumpled against the mattress, panting and smiling and found each other's hands. Their fingers entwined as if they'd never let go.

"Did that happen?" Her voice was like a slow whiskey growl.

"Did what happen?" He rolled to his side and moved her so they faced each other. God, she was beautiful, but never more so than now after making love. Her eyes drooped with passion. Her skin pinked where the trail of his kisses ran from her neck to the apex of her thighs.

"You gave me two."

His chest grew with pride. "I'll give you a hundred more."

She kissed him. "Only a hundred?"

"Maybe you are spoiled and self-centered," he teased. "But if that means I get to make love to you with abandon, I don't care. You name the number and I'll aim to please."

"I won't be selfish," she purred. "I'll always give more than I get."

He kissed her passionately. "You already have, sweetheart. You already have."

They relaxed in each other's arms and once they were clear minded again, they left the bed and showered together. Kevin had purchased a robe for her hoping for just this occasion, an opportunity to wrap her in it. The idea was to move into the kitchen so he could cook, but they didn't make it that far.

CHAPTER TWELVE

Maya

Maya had grown up simply, even though her family was worth a fortune, but she had never known a moment of worry about food or shelter or education. She had the good luck to be born into a family who inherited their wealth from a relative who struck it rich during the Colorado Gold Rush era. She also had the good luck to be born into a family who respected that wealth and didn't squander it despite an indulgence or two.

Even though she hadn't been raised under the veil of the jet set, she brushed elbows with celebrities and the incredibly wealthy just because her prosperity took her to many places and opened many doors.

While her parents played at keeping their children grounded and real, they chose not to raise them among the working-class people of the town that bore the family name.

She wondered if she had grown up in the small town in the way Kevin had, would she regret not having a glitzy lifestyle? There were lots of affluent kids who wore ridiculously expensive shoes and had outrageously expensive houses, but she didn't. While she splurged from time to time, her finances didn't define her. It only solidified people's opinion of her.

She was glad she was here now and overjoyed with Kevin's beautiful present. No sooner had she slipped on the lavender-colored robe did her lover work at taking it off. His hands swam beneath the silkiness to brace her narrow waist. She loved his touch, loved his feel, loved him completely.

She had to fight the impulse to blurt that out, but she had not known him long enough to admit as much. He was not the same polite man that held the door for her. He was now her lover and his primal urges surfaced.

He took her mouth, owning it. He swiftly pushed the robe from her shoulders. She stood before him naked as a Roman statue. He leaned down and wrapped his arms around her hips, lifting her into the air.

Maya laughed hard. She had to be careful because they were both tall and though there was ample ceiling height, there was still the risk of hitting it.

"Duck." He walked through to the living room, where her head skimmed the ceiling then laid her out on the soft sofa and gently ravished her. He rolled her over on her stomach and dotted her spine with kisses.

Her voice vibrated with need. She articulated her pleasure from deep within in long moans and deep throated groans.

He kissed the back of her neck and found other places that stirred her up. She could hardly breathe due to her aroused state. Once again, he turned their bodies so he was right above her, looking deep into her eyes. Deep enough to certainly see her soul.

She reached out her arms and invited him into her. He braced one hand on the armrest of the couch and gripped her hip and slipped inside. This time, both took their sweet, slow time.

The light in the living room was brighter than it had been in the bedroom and she got to see his incredible form in greater detail. He was a fine specimen, she thought with amusement—a beautiful man.

For one so tall and broad-chested, he was surprisingly limber. He arched down to her lips and plunged his tongue inside her mouth. She held his face with her palms and kissed him repeatedly. She pressed her lips to his eyes, to his nose, to his lips before pulling back and simply gazing at his face.

She slid her hands to the small of his back, lifting her hips to counter his rhythm. Her body was primed from the pleasure they'd experienced not so long ago. She was sensitive to every stroke and thrust.

His eyes pressed tight and his jaw strained. He was going to reach his peak and Maya coaxed it forward.

"My goodness," he rasped.

He spoke before she could, but that was all he seemed capable of doing. They were paralyzed as their climaxes washed over them in sweet pulsing waves. Neither wanted to stir until the last of their pleasure had passed. The second they could move, they were up and off the couch, but this time, they stayed dressed in their robes while Kevin put together dinner.

She sat at the breakfast bar while he pan-seared the steaks. The salad was in a bowl on the counter. He was so adept at cooking, and a pleasure to watch. He attacked dinner the way he did everything—with passion and precision.

"It smells wonderful."

He stepped away from the stovetop and kissed her and then poured two glasses of the orange flavored club soda.

Maya rose from the breakfast bar and lit the taper candles he'd set out on the dining room table.

"Is there anything else I can do?" she asked.

He followed her into the dining room and pulled out her chair before kissing her again.

"No. Your job is to sit here and look beautiful. Everything else is done."

He set the salad between them and dished some onto her plate before he served himself. He cut the hot bread and offered her a steaming slice.

"Where did you get this?" She lifted the bread and breathed in the smell as it wafted through the air. Nothing said home like fresh-baked goods. "The grocery store in Idaho Springs is usually out of bread."

He arched an eyebrow and grinned. "You can't buy good bread."

"Really?" She was shocked. "You made this? All the time you slept at John's when we were technically living together, you were making the bread?"

"I cooked for you all the time," he laughed.

"I don't think I realized how much trouble you went through. I must have been out of it." Her head fell forward. "Unbelievable."

"It's okay. That was the past." He buttered a slice and put it to her lips so she could take a bite. She hummed as it melted in her mouth. "This is unbelievable," she moaned.

"Glad you like it."

She sipped her soda. "It's perfect."

"You're easy to please."

"Now you're calling me easy?" she teased.

"I said no such thing. It's taken me almost a year to get you into my bed. That makes you far from easy."

She took another bite of bread. "Had I known." She waggled her brows.

"Everything happens in its own time. Our time finally came."

"Speaking of time, when do I get to see some of these movies of you in action?"

He sat back in his chair and took a deep breath. He hooked his foot on the bottom rung of her chair and dragged her over to him. His house had a great room concept so the kitchen, dining room and living room shared square footage. He grabbed a remote and flipped through files and up popped a football game.

"Oh, my gosh!" she squealed. "That's you! That's you!"

He laughed softly. "Yes."

"Oh my gosh," she said again, this time with bittersweet regret.

"What?"

"I wish we'd lived here. Look at what we missed."

"We always miss something."

He was right; she couldn't be everywhere at the same time.

"I know, but I hated my school." A long breath escaped her. "Let me rephrase. I didn't like it. It wasn't warm and fuzzy. I had no idea this town was so cool."

"That isn't Blackwood." He pointed to the screen and flashed a smile. "That's Mile High Stadium."

"Yeah, but I could have been your girlfriend in high school."

She realized what she had just said. The fact was she and her late husband had been high school sweethearts would mean that she wouldn't have been with Brad. It was an odd mistake for her because it was the first time in a while she hadn't thought about him. Thoughts of him came to her almost daily. She figured she'd had her thought of him for the day now.

She was torn with guilt for having such a great evening.

Rather than pull away like she would have in the past, she huddled tighter against Kevin. He was big and solid and warm. Brad would have liked him. Something settled inside her, and she felt an intense calm wash over her.

"This is so much fun." She watched Kevin on the big screen moving down the field.

"It is." He pressed a kiss to the side of her head. "I thought maybe tomorrow, if you want, I can take you to breakfast. There's a neat place in Idaho Springs. You know, just spend the day together."

"I think that's a wonderful idea, but I'm tired of Idaho Springs, it being my slippery slope and all."

"I thought about that." He thumbed her chin so she would look at him. "There's no better way to fix that than by making good memories there. Having it become a safe place is important. How about pancakes and shopping?"

"Okay." She squeezed his hand. "I'll do anything to spend more time with you." She picked up her phone and texted her brother. "I'm letting Clem know I'm spending the night."

Kevin smiled at her. "Baby, I think he knows."

CHAPTER THIRTEEN

Kevin

Despite it being his day off, Kevin woke at 4:30 a.m. as though he were going to work. He lumbered out of bed naked to start the coffee. He rarely paraded around his house nude. This was definitely a new experience. Standing in his kitchen with the overhead light on and a clear shot out the window to his front lawn, he leaned over the sink and drew the kitchen curtains shut.

Once the coffee was brewing, he climbed back into bed beside the wonderfully warm and naked Maya. It seemed the most natural thing in the world. He was eager and impatient for what was happening between them to become established and irreversible. He would marry Maya if he could, but it was too new and he didn't want to rush things.

Maya backed her body into him. She reached for his arms and wrapped them around her. Even though the house temperature was comfy, the covers were cozy and her body was warm. They snuggled tightly together.

"Coffee smells wonderful," she purred. "Tell me, did you make coffee for me when you lived at John's?"

"I'm hurt you don't remember," he teased.

His hands roamed her body. They cupped her breasts and stroked her stomach until he moved down to her hips. She was ready for him, already writhing and eager. He made slow, quiet love to her. Their bodies were no longer strangers to one another and connected in the most intimate way possible.

Wonderfully sated, they drifted back to sleep. When they woke, they were both rested from their passionate first night together. They packed the coffee for the road and took off toward Idaho Springs for a real breakfast.

There wasn't much in Idaho Springs that they couldn't get in Blackwood, though the reverse could not be said. Idaho Springs was like a movie set version of their town.

Money had moved in a couple of decades prior and it became a faddish, understated hangout for the jet set, but it was still fun to take a field trip there now and again.

"Shall we take your truck or do you wanna drive my car?" Her eyes lit up.

"What's wrong with my truck?" He stole a glance at her.

"Well—nothing," she confessed. "I want to see you drive my Porsche. I think you'd look hot in it. If not this morning, I hope you'll indulge me some time."

"Oh, if you think it would be hot," he teased. "I'm so there."

She tossed the keys to him and Kevin led her to the passenger side to open the door.

The car was a manual shift and he had to admit it was fun to drive.

"I barely touch anything and it goes."

"You're a natural. You look great in the driver seat. It was Brad's car." The words left her lips in a whisper. "Is that okay?"

"It's fine. Don't feel awkward about that." In all truth, he couldn't get upset at her mentioning Brad. The man had been a huge part of Maya's life. He'd been her first love and that deserved a level of respect. Kevin planned to be her second love. That meant he had to leave room for her to work around the feelings she still had for Brad.

"You're so wonderful."

"I'm glad you think so." He turned and gave her a sexy wink.

She tucked her long hair behind her ears and looked out the window. "Where are we going?"

"I thought we'd get breakfast on Colorado Boulevard." He shifted and settled into the butter-soft leather seats. He pushed the gas and the car shot forward. "Maybe we'll do a little window shopping on Miner Street."

"That sounds like fun." She reached over and set her hand on his thigh in such a comfortable always-done-it way. "Something different."

Kevin revved the engine. He could definitely get used to a car like hers. It took nothing to get to Idaho Springs. Racing up the highway with the sun guiding their way, he reflected on how good life was.

Maya tensed when he went too fast. He took her hand and held it in his own to comfort her until he had to shift again.

The sun warmed the early spring morning, which for Colorado still meant sweaters and sometimes snow. He parked her car on the busy street and rushed around to help her out. They walked hand in hand until he pointed to a diner he'd been to years ago. "Here we go. Let's visit Marion's."

The second they stepped in and before they could even focus, a boy of about eleven years old pointed at Kevin.

"Bam Bam." He pounded his chest. "Dad, look."

Maya gazed at Kevin. She smiled from ear to ear.

"I thought the cop was kidding. That's what they called you? Is it some kind of football name or something more like a cartoon character?"

He shook his head and sighed. "Yes. Remember the Flintstones?"

She reached over and squeezed the muscle of his arm. "I can see it. Only your hair is darker."

"It was lighter when I was on the field and in the sun all the time."

The boy charged up to him and hugged him. Most every diner turned to look. Kevin patted the young kid's back.

"Can I have your autograph?" the boy asked.

"Let us sit down first." Kevin pointed to the empty table near the front window. "Go get me something to write with and something to write on."

The boy took off like a sprinter in a race until Kevin shouted, "Walk!"

He held Maya's chair out for her.

A wide smile lit up Maya's face. "Can I have your autograph too?" She rose and kissed him on the cheek before she took a seat.

The boy returned with paper and pen and told him what to write.

"My name is Brian."

Kevin wrote *To Brian, from Kevin Hoisington*.

"Can you put your phone number on it?" Brian pointed to the bottom of the note. "Right here?"

Kevin coolly shook his head. "No, I cannot."

"What about a picture? Can I have a picture with you?"

"Okay. One." Kevin could never say no to a kid. He remembered being a bright-eyed youngster waiting by the exit of the Denver Bronco stadium for anyone to come out and sign his jersey. Somehow, he'd never lost that feeling of wonder or the feeling of gratitude that someone would consider him worthy of their time.

The boy huddled up against him and held out his phone.

"Wait," Maya insisted. "I can take it for you. Is that okay, Brian?"

"Sure. Are you his wife?" Brian asked excitedly.

"No." Maya grinned. "Hold still, you two. Say cheese."

Brian sustained a long 'cheeeeese' until she snapped the photo.

Her eyes softened as she looked at it. "Beautiful," she announced after handing him his phone back.

"Okay." Kevin pointed away from the table to where Brian's parents looked on with happiness. "Back to your parents, young man."

"Thank you." Brian gave him another hug and went back to his table, but he kept an eye on Kevin the whole time.

"You want to take selfies with me too?" he asked.

"I would love a picture of us together." She waved to Brian to come back to the table.

The boy had one speed—fast.

"Walk, buddy," Kevin said in his policeman's voice.

"Can you take a picture of us?" Maya handed him her phone.

Maya and Kevin touched their heads together and smiled. Kevin's head buzzed with the power of their connection. She made him dizzy with joy.

The boy took their picture and handed off her phone, returning to his table at a much slower pace.

"I love it." Maya bounced in her seat like an excited child.

The scent in the air dictated their orders. Maya opted for cinnamon French toast bathed in hot maple syrup. Kevin ordered bacon and eggs.

The great thing about diners was they were generally

good and almost always quick. In a few moments, they were digging in.

After a much-too-big breakfast, they took a leisurely stroll over one block to Miner Street, which was where most of the shops were.

When he suggested taking Maya into town, he thought he wanted to take her shopping to buy her another present and now as they approached Miner Street, he knew exactly where they'd go.

"Let's go in here." He pushed open the door painted with the letters that spelled Antonio's.

It was a high-end, exclusive jeweler. Many of the stores, like the one where Kevin had bought her jacket, might have looked like they were innocuous shops in a touristy Old West town, but they were actually boutiques with big price tags.

"Do a lot of shopping here?" Maya asked dryly.

"Not enough, but you're going to change all that."

"Good morning," the clerk greeted them.

"Hello." Kevin walked into the store like he was a regular. While he wasn't, he never let people or things intimidate him.

Looking at Maya surrounded by sparkling cases of beautiful jewels, he knew this was the right place and the right time. It had been a long time since he'd had a woman he wanted to spoil. He was itching to pamper the hell out of Maya.

"What can I help you with today?" the clerk asked.

"Oh, we're just looking." Maya moved along the display case.

"No," Kevin corrected. "We're not. We're buying."

He pushed back her hair and checked out her ears to see what kind of earrings she wore. Then he looked at her long beautiful neck.

"Maybe a necklace or a pair of earrings?"

"Evin-Kay," she said in Pig Latin.

"I think this fine gentleman can figure out what you're saying."

"It's kind of pricey in here." She gave him one of those serious stares. The kind that almost crossed her eyes.

He let go of a short, sharp laugh. "Are you worried I can't afford it?"

"I didn't say that." She was backpedaling.

"You kind of implied it."

"I meant that I'm a lot more practical, that's all."

"You're driving around in a car worth more than most of the houses in Blackwood."

"I realize that." She wrapped her hands around his thick arm and leaned into his side. "I told you. I'm working on it. Working on a plan for Blackwood."

"Are you going to buy the town back?"

"I might, if I can."

He beamed at her. He could not get over how beautiful she was.

They walked up to a glass case. "Relax." He pressed a kiss to her forehead. "I have money."

She tilted her head to look up at him. "That's cool, but this wasn't a conversation about your ability to buy things. I am practical."

"I know you are, or you think you are, but I want to buy you a present. Let's not be practical this once."

He mulled over the rows of earrings. The amethysts drew his attention. He liked purple on her. The lavender robe, the leather jacket, and now these. He could get hooked on shopping for her.

"Do you like those?" he asked, pointing at the earrings that caught his eye.

"They're beautiful."

"Is this awkward for you?" While Maya could buy herself anything in the store, he knew she wouldn't. That was where her practicality showed.

"It's new," she said honestly.

"Just earrings," he whispered. "For now."

He asked the clerk to pull the amethyst earrings out so he could hold them up to Maya's ears. They were lovely elegant teardrops that would pop against her dark hair and tawny skin.

"Do you like them?"

The clerk had placed a mirror out for her to admire herself, but she was too busy gazing up at him.

"Excuse us." Kevin turned from the clerk and kissed Maya.

She was breathless when he pulled away.

"Yes. I like them." All four words slipped out on an exhale.

"Put them on." There was still the risk of her refusing his gift, but once they were on her ears, he knew she'd keep them.

He gave the clerk his credit card and Maya fitted the earrings into her pierced ears.

"I think it's time for another picture." He signed the slip and then handed his phone to the clerk. "I apologize for the inconvenience," he said. "Would you mind?"

"No." She took hold of his phone and snapped several pictures. "It's so nice to see a couple in love."

Kevin and Maya smiled warmly at her.

He scrolled through to find the best shot. "This one goes on my desk."

CHAPTER FOURTEEN
Maya

Several days after the incident, the police called Maya and asked her to come to the station, which meant another trip to Idaho Springs. This one infinitely less pleasant than breakfast and shopping with Kevin. She didn't understand why she couldn't talk to someone at the Blackwood Police Station, but she cooperated.

The Idaho Springs Police Station was on the same street as the church where the meeting had been held.

She drove by the scene first just to review the incident in her mind. Much to her surprise, though, she wasn't asked to come down to the station to give a statement on the attack.

She was going down to the station because the man had filed charges against Kevin and she had to give her eyewitness account.

The Idaho Springs Police station wasn't much bigger than

the one in Blackwood. Maya entered the stand-alone building and was directed to a conference room.

It surprised her that they actually had her face to face with the man who'd pestered her and grabbed her at the meeting. She took a seat across from him. When the officer introduced her, she remembered so many more details, including his name. Tim Johnson. He was wearing a brace around his neck. She hoped he wasn't faking, and that he needed it.

She texted Deena Grace, the Blackwood Corporation attorney, because she was the only lawyer whose contact information was handy.

"I'm going to ask you to put your cell phone away." The interviewing policeman glared at her.

"I'm texting my lawyer." She was livid and could hardly type because her hands were shaking so bad. She felt a darkness rise within her.

Her eyes met Tim's before she pressed send. "Done." She stared straight at him, hoping her glare delivered the message she was unhappy. "You have some nerve."

Of course, Tim was lawyered up though he couldn't have paid much for his services. His snout-nosed attorney wasn't one for details with his mussed-up hair and sweat-stained shirt. She didn't want to look too closely, but she'd swear the brown spot on the man's tie was gravy.

"Not sure why you called your lawyer. You're not under arrest. We aren't here because you're being charged with anything."

Tim pulled at the brace around his neck. "She thinks because she's a Blackwood, she's entitled to certain privileges."

"You thought because I'm a Blackwood I wouldn't miss the money you stole from me. We have you on tape. The statute of limitations has not run out, and I can press charges tomorrow."

"If you would like to," said the officer, "we can handle that, but in the meantime, we need to focus on the matter at hand."

She had been lying about the tape but Tim didn't know that. Bluffing wasn't her strong suit when she was drunk and she hoped it worked better now that she was sober. There most likely wasn't any way of proving he'd robbed her, but her cousin Cal and brother Clem seemed to think so.

There might be something on the surveillance tapes at her Idaho Springs home or any of her other homes, depending on whether she'd brought him there. With the way Tim and his lawyer flinched, she realized they weren't sure if she was telling the truth or fibbing.

"Tell us what happened."

"Are you asking me or him?" She looked from the officer to Tim. "Why is he in the room? This is a weird set-up. Feels like coercion."

"It's the set-up you have." The officer picked up his pen and laid the tip to the top of the paper in front of him.

"Does Kevin know?" She considered pulling out her phone again to text him. "Shouldn't he be here?"

"We'll get to him."

She would have told Kevin had she known this was the way it was going to go. She'd assumed she'd be making a simple statement and be on her way.

"Real nice of you to ask me to make a statement while the guy who attacked me is staring me down. I would like to speak to you in a different room." She hardly recognized the firmness in her voice.

"If he attacked you, why didn't you make a statement the night he was taken away?" asked the lawyer.

"I went to the hospital the first chance I got, and I believe the x-rays and photos are being filed with this station. It's standard procedure to file a police report in the event of an assault."

"We're playing games here," said the lawyer.

Maya pointed to him. "What's your name?"

"Tyler Brandt."

"I'm not saying anything in front of you." She fisted her bag and stood. "You're playing games." She turned to the officer. "If you want a statement, I'll do it outside. Otherwise, I never want to see this man again. Depending on counsel from my lawyer, I may be pressing charges against you."

The officer held the door for her.

The lawyer blurted, "My client has a right to face his accuser."

"You're making the accusation. If you were being honest, you wouldn't have to keep your story straight." She gave them a smile that wasn't a smile at all. She hoped the smug turn of her lips sent them the message she intended, which was to piss off.

The officer took her into another room. It was small and she was uncomfortable standing so close to him. Better to make her statement quick and get out of there.

"I spoke at an AA meeting and this guy heckled me, and so I left. But I have to back up a bit because there's more to this story." She pressed her memory for anything she could recall about Tim. "I sort of knew him during the last days of my binge drinking, which was over six months ago. My brother and cousin caught him hustling me. Anyway, he chased me out of the meeting and he grabbed me—"

She showed him the bruises.

"He had a strong, painful hold on me. Kevin called out for him to stop, but he ignored him and threatened to take me with him against my will. That's when Kevin charged. This guy had plenty of time to let me go and back away. Kevin gave him a chance and a warning."

The cop nodded.

"Done?" she asked. "Couldn't we have done this over the phone?"

She didn't want to ruin any help she was to Kevin's cause by being snarky. The last thing she needed to do was to appear a spoiled, entitled heiress, but she was angry.

"We generally take statements in person. I apologize for the confusion and inconvenience."

She shook her head. "I'm not sure how this guy knew I

had money, but he did, and he's been after it ever since. He thinks the way to me is through Kevin. Don't indulge him."

She left the conference room only to run into Kevin coming down the hall. He was in his uniform and that had to be a good sign. She sat on the impulse to run up to him and kiss him. She also wanted to apologize, but that would seem like an admission of some kind, and she didn't want to give anyone the satisfaction.

Kevin gave her a look that said *why didn't you tell me you were coming?*

The truth was, she hadn't wanted to trouble him. Everything between them had been so wonderful and she didn't want to mar it with something negative.

Kevin didn't seem fazed by the circumstances, but he was fine-tuned into her.

"Dave." He nodded to the officer she had spoken to. "Let's do this."

Maya panicked even though Kevin was calm.

"See you at home." He kissed her on the cheek.

Maya raced back to Blackwood. She was so angry, she was fevered. She pulled into the driveway of John's house but didn't bother to park in the garage. She headed straight for her laptop. She was crazed to find something that would nail this man.

She called the security company and then she called Clem. He knew that Tim had taken money from her; she needed to know how he knew.

"Are you calling me from the house?" he asked, smiling as

he walked into the office.

"Yes." She looked up at him. "I'm a little anxious."

They set their phones down.

"How did you know the guy I was with before I went to rehab was taking my money?"

"The bank told us," he said casually. "I got a call, and then they forwarded an email with a *do you know this man* alert?"

"How did you get it?"

He looked at her like she was from Mars.

"You don't know?" he asked.

She tilted her head. "Nope, kind of why I'm asking." Her voice was colored with irritation.

"At the end of your run, you were having issues with gambling. The corporation could be compromised because you were dipping into your trust pretty heavily. We set up an account that gave you reasonable living expenses apart from your trust. He was cashing checks from your living expense account." Clem lifted his shoulders. "Since I was the trustee of that account, I got the notices. You got notified too. You probably have a copy of it in your emails somewhere. They should be archived."

She did a search and found a bunch of unopened emails. She nearly hit the ceiling when she found what he described. Tim Johnson had taken a lot of money. It hurt to realize just how compromised she had been. She immediately sent everything to Kevin's phone.

Kevin called back immediately. "You found something?"

"Yes, I want to get this guy," she insisted. "I don't want anything to happen to you."

"I'm fine. I'm done with the inquiry. The guy couldn't keep his story straight and the church had surveillance, but I'll turn over the things you sent. You can still press charges if you want. You may have to once they get the doctor's report. He assaulted you."

She let out a sigh. "I want you to come home."

She didn't want to sound like a whiner, but she needed the comfort of his arms. She'd gone through the gamut of emotions at the police station. She needed Kevin. "I'm all stressed out. I just want normal. It's lunchtime. Wanna go to the diner?"

"Yes, baby. I want to go there."

Maya felt like she'd been all over creation by the time she walked out to her car.

Another car was coming up the remote road that led to John's driveway.

She stepped back because she didn't recognize it. As the driver opened the door and let daylight into her car, there was Kaitlin, Clem's soon to be ex-wife, behind the wheel, looking less than happy.

Clem was in good spirits this morning. She didn't want to ruin that with a visit from his ex, but as long as Kaitlin was civil, she'd let her in.

Maya hugged her hello. She'd always liked her sister-in-law and though it was strange that soon she would be a former sister-in-law, she hoped there would be a way to stay on good terms.

When Kaitlin pulled back, tears were running down her cheeks.

"Where's Clem?" Her voice quivered with emotion.

"Inside." Maya looked over her shoulder toward the front door. "Come on in. I'll let him know you're here."

She led the sobbing woman to the couch and then dashed upstairs to get her brother. Life was too complicated these days. She knocked on Clem's door, hating to bother him.

He answered half-dressed with wet hair. "What's up?"

"Kaitlin's here."

Clem rubbed his face with his palm. "Tell her I'll be down." His voice wilted with every word, but he moved like he was excited.

"Need me to stay?" She prayed he'd say no, but she would if he needed her.

"No, I do not," he said sharply.

"Hey," she reprimanded him softly. "Maybe I should if you're going to be nasty."

"I'm sorry. I'm fine. I'll be civil. I promise."

"Good, because she's crying." She reached over and pushed the damp strands of hair from her brother's forehead. "She looks a mess, so go easy on her."

Clem's expression turned to one of concern. "Can you stay until I see what's going on?" He walked back to his bed where his shirt was laid out and pulled it on. "You and I haven't talked about what happened between Kaitlin and me." He tugged on his boots and walked to the door. "There's been some game playing."

"No," teased Maya. "Really?"

"Yes, I'm not proud of it," he said. "Can you stay for a few?"

"Sure."

"I'll be right down." He headed for the bathroom.

She had flexibility, so she went downstairs to sit with Kaitlin until Clem came down.

"How about you let me get you a glass of water?"

Kaitlin's eyes moved around the great room like she was lost. Maya sat her down on the couch and took off her shoes. She lifted her feet and encouraged her to curl up on the sofa while Maya covered her with a plush blanket.

"Get comfortable. You've been in that car for a while." She loved her brother but hated to see his wife so broken. "I'll get you that water."

Clem sauntered down the stairs as Maya returned with a full glass. She could see the hope on his face. It reminded her of when they were kids and they raced down to open presents on Christmas morning. He tried to filter his excitement, to slow it down, but she knew her brother. He was wishing for something specific.

"I think we'll be okay," assured Clem. "Right, Kaitlin?"

"Yes." Her voice was weary.

"I'm only a phone call away," Maya promised. "I'm going into town to have lunch with Kevin. I can come back if you need me."

As soon as she was sure that Kaitlin and Clem were good, she raced to her Porsche and sped down to Blackwood. She'd spent more time in the town in the past few months than she had when she owned the place.

She parked legally and rushed inside.

Togi's arms were filled with plates balanced from her wrist to the crook of her elbow, a coffee pot dangling from her fingertips. She was a welcome sight. Once she delivered the load, Maya gave her a hug hello.

"Can I grab a booth?" Maya pointed to the empty one.

"Yep." Togi followed Maya with a pot of coffee as she scurried to a table and slid into a polished wooden bench. "You look wound up."

"I am. I just got back from the Idaho Springs Police Station. That guy who did this"—she pointed to her wrist— "is trying to get Kevin for police brutality."

"They should have had us all down there to talk to them right away." Togi turned over Maya's cup and filled it.

Maya could feel Togi's toughness flaring.

"You should be in charge." She lifted her cup and took the first sip. "It was such a weird experience. I'm going to tell Kevin about it when he gets here. It was almost like the officer asking me questions was working for the man."

"What do you mean?" Togi set the coffee pot down and slid into the bench across from her.

"I don't know." She shook her head. "Maybe it's me being paranoid, but I couldn't shake this feeling like they were trying to work together to get a payday. The officer seemed smarmy but then he apologized."

"Does that happen a lot? People trying to angle for your money?"

"I guess." She hadn't given it much thought until Tim showed back up. "I wasn't aware of it when my husband was alive. Once I was single, the vultures came out of the woodwork. I think they're still trying to get a piece of what I have."

Kevin walked in shortly after and Maya's heart soared.

Togi rose and grabbed her pot.

Kevin leaned down and kissed Maya on the lips before sitting down across from her.

"Hi, Togi."

"Cup of coffee?" She held the pot handle with two fingers and swung it back and forth. The dark liquid danced behind the glass.

"Yes, ma'am."

She turned over his cup and poured.

"Do you guys know what you want or do you need a minute?" Her eyes swept the dining room. It wasn't busy, but there was a decent crowd.

"Give us a minute." Kevin politely dismissed her.

And with that, Togi was off to check her other customers.

A big wave of relief swept through her now that Kevin was there. She'd just seen him and yet she was excited to see him again. Was he her new addiction?

"You remain at large?" she giggled.

"I do."

"Why was that cop so gung-ho? It was almost like he was working for them." She picked up her napkin and turned it into confetti. It was a bad habit she needed to break because it made such a mess. "I didn't need to face those guys like that. I couldn't shake the feeling they all had dollar signs in their eyes, like they were after my money."

"I think if they could get to your money, they would, but they were after mine, not yours."

"*Yours?*" she asked with surprise.

He laughed heartily. "Believe it or not, I'm flush. I have money from playing ball. You were right, there was some shady stuff going on there, but we're square. I told my captain on the way out."

"It's done?"

He shrugged. "Let's hope." He reached across the table for her hand. "I do have one question—"

"Yes?" She looked at her hand sitting on his palm. How his fingers brushed over her knuckles. How the light feeling of his touch made her heart pound in her chest.

"Why are you sitting way over there?" His voice took on that velvet bedroom quality.

She let his warm words wash over her.

"From this distance, you can admire my beautiful earrings." She tucked her hair behind her ears. "This handsome, wonderful man gave them to me."

"I think I remember something about that." He gave her hand a tug. "Come over here."

She smiled and slipped over to his side of the booth. They barely fit side-by-side but his close proximity was perfect.

Togi approached the table. "Can I start you off with anything?"

"I'd like an Arnold Palmer, coleslaw, and a side of fries."

Togi arched her brow, signaling her disapproval over the order.

Maya didn't respond.

Kevin ordered a grilled chicken salad and handed Togi the menus. "Are you going to let her order that crap, Togi?"

"Ugh, you two." Maya searched for an alternative order.

"Eat what you like," murmured Togi. "What do I care if your ass gets as wide as a bus eating all those fries?"

Maya grumbled. "Okay, make that two grilled chicken salads."

Togi smiled and marched away to put their order in.

Maya leaned into Kevin. "I talked to Deena about the developer and she called me counselor, like I sounded like an attorney."

There was a pause. She looked to him for a response.

"Is that something that interests you?"

"I was flattered, that's all. I haven't done anything with myself. I got a degree in design, and then I got married. I want to do something meaningful like you do."

He nodded and leaned over to kiss her. "Everything you do is meaningful."

She rolled her bottom lip between her teeth. "What do

you think about me seeing if I can buy the town back?" she asked quietly.

He studied her and smiled. "I like that idea." He sipped his coffee. "Clem expressed regret about selling it too. I'd kind of like to keep it as it is."

"It's just an idea. I'm going to make sure one way or the other the development company makes good on preserving everyone's jobs like they promised."

"See there, you're doing worthwhile work already."

Togi appeared with their food. It took no time to fix the salads.

Maya felt like Togi wanted to ask her something. "What is it?"

Togi looked around the diner then leaned in close. "There's a meeting this evening here at the town hall. I'd be honored if you led."

"Are you sure? It was a major disaster the last time."

Togi nodded. "True, but not your fault. Besides, it would give everyone a chance to get to know you. Make you part of our group. Your sponsor is big on service."

Maya studied her for a minute. "Okay, I'll do it."

She looked up and Kevin gave her a dopey smile.

"What?" she giggled.

"That's what I call being of service."

"Glad you think so. If I can give back, I'm happy to."

"See there, if you don't like the environment, then be a positive change in it. Those people were there for you when you could barely stand on your own. Now you can do that for someone else just starting out."

"You're right."

He was quiet and then made a confession. "I heard you."

"What's that?" She poured oil and vinegar on the big salad.

"The other night when you shared at the meeting. I was outside waiting for you. I was so excited to tell you how I felt. Then I heard you share. You have a great story. You have a lot to give."

"I thought the people in Blackwood hated me. You saw how they were the other day when I asked her to be my sponsor." She stabbed the chicken with vigor. "I was wrong. Just shows you how wrong you can be. Like I didn't think you liked me any other way than just as a friend."

"There, you were way off base. I'm just saying no one is perfect. You gotta sift through the shit sometimes."

"You're wrong. You're perfect," she countered.

"I'm not." He smiled into his coffee. "But I like being in a relationship with you."

"Can we be official?" she asked affectionately.

"It's a done deal, sweetheart. You were mine the day I laid eyes on you, only you didn't know it then."

"Anything else you know that I don't?"

Kevin gave her a devious smile she couldn't dig into since Togi appeared and set a ticket down on their table top.

"I'm just clocking out for the day. Take your time."

Maya pulled out her credit card. "Go ahead and run it so I can give you your tip."

"Aw honey, I'm in no hurry."

"Go ahead so you can close out before you leave." She pressed her card into Togi's hand.

Togi left and reappeared.

"Thanks, folks. See you tonight."

She added the tip and signed it.

Kevin shook his head. "You and Clem with your hundred-dollar tips."

"I don't do it all the time." She tucked the card and receipt into her purse. "However, if I can get away with it, I will."

CHAPTER FIFTEEN

Kevin

Kevin kissed his beautiful girlfriend goodbye and set out to patrol Blackwood. He could hardly focus on his surroundings, being preoccupied with his amazing situation. He replayed every moment he'd spent with Maya.

Reality set in when his radio hissed.

He answered with a "This is Kevin."

It was Damon again and another Blackwood was at the saloon, very upset. This time it was Clem.

"Has he had too much to drink?" He talked into the radio with one hand and steered with the other.

"I didn't serve him. I'm not sure what's going on. He's emotional and he's asking for you."

"I'll be right there."

Kevin pulled out of one parking lot and into another. He parked the cruiser and strolled into the saloon, which had only a handful of customers. He leaned on the bar next to Clem, whose forehead sat heavily against the wooden surface of the bar.

"What's going on?" Kevin asked quietly. There was no need to spread anyone's dirty laundry around town.

He lifted his head. Clem's forehead was red where the blood had pooled. "Kaitlin," he gasped. "She wants to get back together."

He made sure Clem couldn't see him when he rolled his eyes.

"That's a good thing, right?"

"If someone had said my wife wanted to get back together a month after she left me, I would have embraced it, but I just walked through hell." He rubbed at his bloodshot eyes. "She left me nearly a year ago. I was seeing the light. Just getting used to a life without her."

"Do you love her?"

Clem nodded. "I do," he replied like he was reciting his wedding vows. "I can't do this again. I can't take the risk. I don't even know if she's sure."

"Take it slow. Maybe this goes nowhere. You're upset right now because you think you have to sort it out immediately. You don't have to know right now. Nothing's changed. You're safe, you're sound, and now you have more options."

Clem smiled and then he laughed. "You have got to be the most rational person I've ever met." He offered his hand for Kevin to shake. "I get what you're saying. I gotta find a job.

I'm climbing the wall in that big house. It's so damn …
empty."

"Don't I know it. Caleb has one just like it," laughed
Kevin. "Speaking of… Deena is talking to Maya about the
development company and Maya is considering buying back
the town."

A wicked smile spread across his lips.

"That's interesting. So am I."

"Geez, you guys live in the same house. Maybe you
should talk." Damon dropped off two cups of coffee and
walked away. "The developer has dropped the ball. You and
Maya can sort that out so you don't get consumed with
Kaitlin. It'll keep your head clear, or at least busy."

"Good idea," said Clem. "Thanks again."

"Hey, Clem." Kevin picked up his coffee and took a sip.
No use wasting the gift. "I'm happy to help out." He reached
into his pocket and pulled out his business card. "Let's do
this a different way if you need something again. Call me
directly."

"Sure thing, man. Sorry."

"No worries."

Clem stood up and something occurred to Kevin. He
gritted his teeth. "You rode your bike again, didn't you?"

Clem hung his head. "Yes."

"Dammit," scolded Kevin.

"Sorry," he said with a shrug and a laugh.

"I'm serious. I'll charge you next time. If I could do that

now, I would, but I have to find a reason. You shouldn't ride a bike on I70. It's too dangerous. Don't do it again."

His phone buzzed with a text from Maya. Her cousin-in-law Deena was coming to town to meet about the sale.

"Hey, Clem. Maya is meeting about the sale of the town. Do you want to go?"

Clem's whole demeanor changed. Moments ago, he was pounding his head against the bar in frustration. Now he was slapping his palms against the surface in excitement.

"I can take you over to where they're meeting but promise me no more bike riding. They're calling for a late spring snow."

"I'm good," he promised. "It just comes in waves, and I can't handle it."

"We can walk over to the town hall and you can keep your bike at the station again until I can bring it over to the house in my truck." He narrowed his eyes at Clem. "You have a car, use it."

As they passed the bar, Clem shook Damon's hand. "I apologize if I was any trouble."

"We're cool."

Kevin bumped fists with Damon. "Catch you later."

He and Clem walked out of the bar.

CHAPTER SIXTEEN

Maya

Maya watched patiently as the Blackwood Corporation lawyer Deena Blackwood, who was a newlywed to her cousin Caleb, snagged a room in the town hall to lay everything out for her. She wanted to go over all she'd found out after reviewing the progress the developer had made since the sale of Blackwood.

Deena brought two copies of a stack of papers with post-it flags on them pointing out the areas in which the development company that had purchased the town was now in default.

Kevin and Clem knocked on the door as she started. Maya wondered if she'd ever tire of seeing him. Would her heart continue to race each time he was near?

"You going to join us?" she asked him.

He winked and they smiled at each other. They must have

stared too long as both Deena and Clem cleared their throats.

"Sorry," Maya said bashfully.

"Gotta go check in on my mom's neighbor. I'm going to get her snow shovel out in case we need it. Probably toss salt on her sidewalk as a precaution. After that, I'll be at the station. I've got desk duty." He kissed her goodbye. "You all have fun. Talk to you later."

Deena drew a visual line from Kevin to Maya and smiled. "Okay then." She raised her perfectly plucked eyebrows.

"I'm so happy." Maya smiled. "Over the moon happy. I mean, he's going to salt someone's walkway. How can you not love that?"

"Love?" Deena and Clem chorused.

"Feels like it," she gushed. "Imagine that." She shrugged. "Whatever it is, he feels the same way, and I'll take happy over heartache any day."

"I'm glad for you, sweetie." Deena patted her hand. "He's a nice man."

Without warning, Deena suddenly made a face and dashed out of the room. She returned disheveled and pulled out a pack of crackers from her purse.

"Caleb's cooking," Deena laughed as Maya eyed her suspiciously.

Clem sat next to Maya and listened. She gave her brother a cursory glance and thought he looked like a wreck. She didn't know what to think since he'd been making so much progress.

Deena, mid-first sentence of her analysis, got up and took a box of tissues from a side table in the meeting room and handed it to Clem.

"What I propose is to have a family meeting. I think it's critical to let everyone know what's going on. The two of you have expressed seller's remorse. It's possible other members of the family are feeling this too. There is a catch, though, and everyone should be there."

Deena paused and looked at Clem.

"What?" he asked.

"I know you and Kaitlin are having issues." Deena swallowed hard and reached for a packet of crackers. "Even so, she's still a member of the corporation and until that changes, she has to be present. Is that going to be a problem?" She tore open the wrapper and readied the cracker to eat. "I think the best place to have it would be at our house or John's since they're both big enough to hold the family."

"I don't care." Clem looked to the floor. "What's one more time?"

"Okay. I'll set it up. I think it's a good idea to meet and get our ducks in a row. You know, see where everyone is regarding this situation. I think the development company got in over its head and while no one in Blackwood Corporation has an obligation to step in, it could."

"How much money are we talking about?"

"The same or less than what the corporation put out, but in order for the corporation to take it back, everyone has to be on board. If, say, Caleb or John or Patrick or your sister

Jennifer don't want to play along, you could still buy it back, but it would come out of your personal pockets."

"What if we got the corporation to buy it back and then we paid off anyone who didn't want to be involved? Could we work something like that out? It could be cheaper to reacquire as a group," said Clem.

"Usually I don't advise that sort of thing with families, but your family might be the exception. I honestly never saw one, even an extended family, where there is absolutely no bad blood between anyone. However, this could change that."

"That's why we need to have a meeting," said Clem. "Let's have it at John's, since it's just the two of us—Maya and me—and you guys might not want to host all of us. I'll take care of it."

"I can contact Kaitlin if you want." Deena took a few bites of a cracker.

"Good luck finding her."

Maya gasped. "She was just here. What happened?"

"She doesn't know what she wants." His eyes brimmed with tears. "She came all the way out here to see me because she had to have me. Then she got here and after we spent the night together, she wasn't so sure. Now she's ghosted on me again."

"That's weird." She'd felt sorry for her sister-in-law, but now she was annoyed. She couldn't stand seeing her brother get jerked around.

Deena advised, "You didn't ask, but I'm telling you, this

happens a lot. I can look it up, but if you guys spent the night, the clock might start all over for separation purposes. Cohabiting means that. If you don't want to stay married, you guys have to knock that stuff off."

"I'm here and she's wherever she hides," grumbled Clem. "If you want to call her, that's fine. I just need a ride home. I got bike busted by Kevin again."

"You didn't," scolded Maya. "Now I'm mad at both you and Kaitlin."

"Okay, you two. Back to the family meeting. It's the beginning of the week." Deena looked at her calendar. "You guys want to do Friday night?"

"Yeah," she said, her voice tinged with annoyance. "That works."

"I'll set it up."

"Thanks for doing this."

They all rose to leave.

"You don't have to thank me; you guys pay me." She grinned then shoved the rest of the cracker into her mouth. Deena's complexion turned green and she dashed off again.

"Caleb's cooking my you-know-what," grumbled Maya.

They stepped out of the building and were pelted with snowflakes. The light flurries were almost disappointing since the spring temperatures had been so warm and inviting. Already, green shoots poked through the ground and leaves budded on the trees, signaling new beginnings.

In Blackwood, it could snow well into the next month,

they all knew that, but this was the point at which they got their hopes up annually for clear weather.

"Oops." Deena reappeared. "I need to get home. I don't want to be out in this if it hits hard."

"Drive carefully." Maya suspected she was driving for two, but she didn't want to say if Deena hadn't announced anything.

She turned to her brother.

"I'm driving you home." She marched to her car, calling to Clem over her shoulder. "Seriously, you have a perfectly good car. Use it."

They climbed into the Porsche and headed outside of town to John's house. After some quiet time inside, she found Clem in the living room and spoke to him again. This time with gentleness and compassion.

"If you want to talk about what happened, I'm here for you." She plopped onto the couch beside him.

"I appreciate that." He looked around the room. His eyes rose to the beamed ceiling before they met hers. "I like being here. I like the people, especially Kevin. He's the best. I feel like I can work through anything here."

"You're going to stay?"

"That's the plan." He smiled a rare smile. "It's nice to have a plan."

The snow fell harder but then it stopped. She remembered that she had agreed to lead the meeting, but this time, it would be different. It would be close by, and it would be sane.

"I'm taking a catnap because I have a meeting tonight back at town hall." She lifted from the sofa and walked to the stairs. "Are you sure you're okay?"

"All good."

"Great" She gave him a big hug and climbed the stairs to her room.

She was ready for a nap, but when she got to her room and closed the door, she felt lonely for Kevin. She snuggled into her warm comforter with her phone and texted him.

How is the salt going?

His reply was immediate.

Done. I had to eat some of her cookies though. If I keep being this helpful, I'm going to get fat.

She tried to imagine Kevin fat but couldn't.

Doubtful. But if you're worried, I can help you burn calories.

She imagined him reading her message. Imagined his smile.

Goodness.

She missed him.

It's an open meeting tonight. You're welcome to come.

She watched the dots move across her screen as he replied.

I might. I hear they have a really inspiring speaker tonight.

She lifted up her sweater and bared her breast. She held her phone up and took a picture. It was a shadowy shot so it wasn't an obviously naked picture. She hovered over the send button for a second before she pressed it.

MAYA He wrote back in all caps. **I'm at work. Have a heart**.

She laughed and shot off another text before she put down her phone.

Adore you.

Her nap was quick. She freshened up and went down to enjoy a fire in the living room to gather her thoughts.

Clem came down to join her. His rumpled hair said he'd napped too.

"I'm ready when you are."

"Ready for what?" she asked with a smile.

"To listen to my baby sister talk at her meeting."

"Aww," she said. "Let's go."

CHAPTER SEVENTEEN

Kevin

Kevin wasn't a Blackwood. He wasn't a part of the Blackwood Corporation that used to own the town they inherited, but he was invited to the family gathering just the same. It felt right being there. He prepared for the meeting all week, helping with housework and food preparation. He and Clem moved chairs from various bedrooms to furnish the living room.

"This place looks good with furniture in it," John laughed.

"We can keep it this way," said Clem.

Once everyone had a place to sit comfortably, they rested and munched on the snacks put out for them. Kevin sat next to Maya on the sofa.

When John and Lucy entered the living room, an invisible current of awkwardness sparked. John looked Kevin's way and gave him a nod. Lucy waved. Maya was distracted and didn't seem to notice.

Seeing Lucy made him feel foolish. Like Maya, he had a period in his life when he felt empty. Lucy Shoemaker was a crush he'd had since he was small. When he returned from the pros, she was alone and so was he. He watched after her. Nothing came of it. Still, it was awkward.

Maya wasn't aware that Kevin had had it bad for the woman who'd married her cousin. It went right to the top of his list of things to talk to her about when they were alone.

Lucy broke the ice and said hello. "Hey, Kevin," she said graciously. "Nice to see you, and Maya too."

Maya stood and hugged her cousin-in-law hello. After their less than pleasant first meeting, they'd been cordial and supportive of one another.

John and Kevin shook hands. They had come to terms with one another just as John and Lucy got serious, but there were rough patches in between. Maya seemed to sense the strangeness in the air.

"What's going on?" she whispered.

"We'll talk." Kevin patted her thigh.

Deena and Caleb arrived, Patrick and then Jennifer showed up next. The last holdout was Clem's estranged wife Kaitlin.

"I emailed her." Deena gave Clem a look of sympathy.

"I'm here," Kaitlin called out as she walked through the door. "Sorry. It was snowing on the way in. I had to drive slower than I expected."

"It's not snowing now, is it?" asked John.

"No. I came in from Aspen."

"In *your* car?" scolded Clem. "That's not a good idea."

John put his hand out to stop them. "Not here, guys."

Kevin's heart lifted. He watched Clem's eyes glom onto Kaitlin. Something told him that even though they had their troubles, he had hope they could figure it out.

She was a pretty, petite woman with sweeping blond hair. He could see the reason for the attraction and was rooting for them.

"Okay," said John, who was the oldest of the cousins. "As we all know, there are a few things the people who bought the town have failed to deliver. We have an opportunity to take it back. I personally don't want to do that because Lucy and I have moved to Idaho Springs, and we are working on some other philanthropic projects. My fear is we'll get spread too thin. However, I'm willing to lend financial support if needed. Lucy is now a member of the corporation and can answer for herself. He looked toward her.

She laughed. "At one time I would have jumped at the opportunity to stay in Blackwood. It's always been my home, but I learned something valuable when you sold it. Home is not always a place. My home is wherever John is." She turned to her husband and smiled. "Besides, now that we're running the new non-profit that puts art supplies in the hands of children, we don't have much free time. What little we have I want to spend with John." She smiled. "We are newlyweds."

John wrapped his arm around Lucy's waist. "If there's a

way to work it out so whoever wants it back can have it back without obligating us then I'm all ears."

Caleb seconded John. "I'm not interested either," he said simply and flashed a perfect smile. "Deena?"

"I'm not sure. If I was single, I'd say no, but now that children are a consideration, it's a cool legacy or it could be."

"We had the town as kids, and we didn't appreciate that," added Caleb.

Deena smiled from ear to ear. "Now we have a chance to change that."

Caleb tilted his head.

"I knew it!" Maya squealed.

"What?" Caleb asked.

Deena raised her brows and waited. Everyone in the room got it but Caleb. Each person took a turn miming hints at him, but he was clueless until Deena rocked a phantom baby and hummed a lullaby.

Caleb staggered backward, grabbing the fireplace mantel for balance.

"Wow." John leaned over and steadied him.

"Aww, honey," said Deena. "You okay, Daddy?"

Caleb reached out to her and they hugged.

"I wanted to break the news while everyone was here."

Maya got up and got everyone a glass. She poured so that they could toast.

"Sorry, guys. No alcohol but we have sparkling water."

"That's perfect," said Deena.

Everyone clinked glasses and congratulated the couple.

"Okay." Deena picked up a pen and grabbed her notepad once the toasts were over. "No for Caleb because he will be spending his time learning how to be a stellar daddy. No for John and Lucy. Clem and Maya are interested in taking the town back. My feeling is if the new owners don't get it together, the price will be good. I say we sit back and track this."

"Okay," said Clem.

Maya and Kevin collected all the glasses and brought them to the sink. Maya happened to glance out the window and see the snow. It was coming down hard. This was no longer a flurry but a full-on storm, and that meant everyone was spending the night or the meeting needed to be over now.

"Snow," she said and everyone scrambled.

"Wait." Kaitlin's voice was filled with panic.

Kevin took Maya by the hand and they quietly made their way toward the door.

"Kaitlin, stay in my room." Maya looked around the space. "Everyone, we're leaving. We'll be over at Kevin's. Make yourself at home in John's house."

"That's it?" asked John. "That's our meeting?"

"Yep." She walked back and gave everyone a hug while Kevin waited patiently. "Eat and party and have fun."

He was eager to get her alone. They shuffled in the newly fallen snow. He opened the door for her and hoisted her inside his truck. Maya practically flew in.

He had Clem's bike in the back. Before he forgot, he lifted it out and rolled it into the house and through to the garage.

"Sorry, guys. I don't have the remote." He pointed to Clem. "No riding this. Good night."

He hustled out to the driver's side and climbed in. He was shivering because he'd handled the cold frame of the bike. He touched her cheek with chilled fingers and listened to her shriek.

He leaned in and kissed her. It was so romantic to kiss her while the snow was falling outside around them. The security light shone through the falling flakes, making the snow appear glitter-like as they drove the private road quietly to Blackwood.

The truck glided on I-70, and Kevin thought of Clem riding his bike on this road. There wasn't a lot of traffic as a rule, but most people drove way too fast. He thought of it when Clem first mentioned that he was suicidal, and that he felt that way over a woman he loved.

Kevin wondered if he would feel that way if his heart was broken. He chanced a glance at Maya and knew he would.

She was quiet. The only show of emotion was a slight smile on her face.

"What are you thinking about?"

"Caleb is going to be a dad," she said wistfully.

"Neat, right?"

"Yes. I guess pretty soon John will be a dad too. It happens like that. Pregnancy is contagious. Lucy will want a baby too."

"Did you know that I knew Lucy before I knew you?" It was a good time to mention it.

"She lived here, so I'd assume you knew her."

His confession seemed juvenile since what he felt for Lucy paled in comparison to the strength of emotion he felt for Maya. Comparing the two women was like comparing apples to oranges. Cats to dogs. Night to day. He attacked his admission the same way he removed a Band-Aid—quick and painless. "I had a thing for her," he said, almost embarrassed. "Nothing ever came of it. I cared for her. I thought you should know."

Maya was quiet before she responded, "In truth, Togi mentioned it once, but I didn't think much of it. Did you love her?"

"I thought I did, but she wanted nothing to do with me. I kind of watched over her, and accepted that she didn't want me and that was fine. But because it was the decent thing to do, I tried to take care of her."

"Oh, so you have a long history."

"I suppose. It went back to when we were kids." He lifted his shoulders. "I can't explain it."

"Okay," she repeated, her voice insecure. "Do you have a hard time seeing her with John?"

"No." There was no hesitation with his answer.

"Are you sure?"

"Yes," he replied. "I cared for her, and I thought she needed someone. I couldn't be happier for her or for me." He took her hand and lifted it to his lips. "You're the woman for me."

"You like caring for people, don't you?" she asked with a warm smile.

He nodded and reached over to stroke her cheek softly with his fingers.

It was a good thing they left when they did. He took the Blackwood exit and slowed down. The snow was powdery and the breeze picked up and blew it around like a dust storm. He drove down Main Street, past the saloon. Even though he wasn't on the clock, he always kept his eyes open.

Finally, they arrived at his home. He backed his truck into his driveway just so far, pressed the remote that lifted the garage door, and rolled all the way in.

He took her hand. In the glow of the overhead light, he asked, "Do you want children one day?"

"Yes."

"I want children too. I'm happy for Caleb and Deena." Warmth flooded his heart. "You're right. Bringing up the subject makes me think about kids, and I want them very much."

He helped her out of the truck. Despite the cold of the falling snow, he was warm and relaxed. His feelings for Maya grew. Before he turned the key to the house, he framed her face with his hands and kissed her.

He pressed his lips against hers and slipped his tongue into her warm, wet mouth. In contrast to the cold, she was hot.

She moaned as their lips ground gently against one another. He put his key into the door, reaching around her, drawing her against his body as he opened it. They danced into the entryway of his home, a small rancher that opened into a great room. He had a feeling they would not get much beyond the couch.

He led her to the sofa. She watched as he built them a fire. His fireplace was not like John's, which used both gas and wood. His was fueled by nature alone.

The logs were stacked neatly, the fireplace always cleaned after each fire. He lit the kindling with the lighter. It took a bit, but he was an expert at building fires and the flames caught quickly. He set the lighter back in its place and joined her on the couch.

With his arms wrapped around her he said, "I do want children." He stared at the dancing flames.

"Do you want them with me?" she asked shyly.

He looked to her and hoped the love he felt would show in his eyes. "Yes."

"I know it seems fast, but Kevin ... we've known each other for the better part of the year. Sure, I had to get back on my feet, but I've had a thing for you for a while."

He slid a strand of hair that strayed across her forehead back into line.

"I've had a thing for you as well. And it's not just because I like taking care of people. This is different and it's special."

They sat, embracing each other, gazing at the fire. First, he kicked off his shoes and then she did. When they turned to each other, they fixed their mouths into a slow, savoring kiss. His hands swept her body slowly, finding her buttons so he could remove her shirt.

She took over unfastening as he drew his hands down her hips and lifted her thigh up and over his to straddle him. His palms sat high on her firm thighs.

She was fit with her crazy rope jumping. He'd heard her once when he'd been in the living room at John's, before he moved back home. She'd left the door to the gym open and was going a mile a minute with that rope. She was good at it and he knew it wasn't an easy thing to do because that was one exercise they did for football.

He smiled against her lips, remembering that in all the time he spent with her, they had not worked out together. He would change that right away.

He stroked her from her hips down to the back of her thighs repeatedly. Finally, he encouraged her to rise so he could remove her jeans. She gazed up into his eyes with adoration and wonder. Her expression said everything about how she felt and he felt the same. They were in love.

There was a level of anxiety about the timing and the telling of his love for her. They'd known each other for a respectable amount of time and most of that time was spent together. He'd seen her through hard times, but even connecting on a daily basis, he wanted more. And yet, he debated with himself. Did he expect to meet another woman he would feel this way about? When was the right amount of time before telling her he loved her?

Her blouse was opened and elegantly draped around the full, round perfection. She was naturally beautiful—so blessed. He lifted her flesh with his fingertips and suckled her.

It was as if he had never tasted such sweetness. His tongue bathed the petal soft skin until it peaked. He toyed with the tip as it formed in his mouth.

She clutched his head firmly, her body stiff with tension.

His head so close to her chest, he heard her moan begin as a low growl inside her. He chuckled softly. "Wildcat," he murmured.

Without any other signal, she pushed on his shoulder and urged him back. They shifted positions and she worked to lower his pants. It was clear what she intended. That had not happened to him in some time. He lifted his hips to help her ease his jeans free.

He was hard, and his length lifted the loose cotton of his fitted boxers. The soft strands of her hair splayed around his stomach as she lowered her head.

Her lips were scorching hot on his sensitive skin as she took him completely into the velvet of her mouth. One hand clutched her head, the other the back of the couch as he held on for dear life, enjoying the pleasure she gave him.

His breath sucked in and his eyes closed. He fought for control. He wasn't sure how much he could take before he had to be inside her. He played with her silky strands, fingering them over and over while immense pleasure built within him. He tapped out.

She lifted her head and bore a wicked, pleased-with-herself smile. As if they had the same plan, she crawled forward and he leaned back. Kevin reached for his jeans and pulling out a condom. She rolled it onto him, then lifted up. She steadied herself on the back of the couch and pushed up with her long powerful legs so that she could lower her body onto his length.

She let her weight sink onto his massive frame, pulling him into her as deeply as she could go. They both growled like animals as their bodies were joined completely.

She was everything he could hope for in a woman. He considered himself a lucky man to have found her.

Her lips curled with a hazy smile as she looked at him with heavy-lidded eyes.

"You're so damn beautiful," he told her.

She lowered her face to his in a graceful gliding motion and kissed him with such passion, he thought he would burst within her. He clutched her head, her hair a messy cloud as he deepened the kiss, tasting her, tagging her, owning her.

He moved his lips from hers to the dip in her collarbone, bracing himself for the pleasure that was about to hit. His breath hot against her skin caused her body to tense. A gasp of pleasure left her lips before she pulsed powerfully around him. Her pleasure triggered his and soon he was helplessly following her over the cliff.

He rolled, bracing her so they were side by side. When he regained his senses, he covered her face with kisses.

"Mmm," he said again.

"Mmm, indeed."

The fire crackled beside them, sending the shadows of light dancing across the cream-colored walls.

Moments later, they rose and went their separate ways, freshening up before taking a place in front of the fire. He stoked the flames, adding another log before sitting back. She lay down in between his body and the hearth. They admired the warmth and the beauty of the simple scene in front of them.

"I love you," he confessed.

She pulled his arm tightly around her. "I love you too."

"I got so worried about what people would think, whether I was rushing things or what. The truth is, I don't think I could find a more perfect woman than you. I don't—"

She rolled around and touched his lips.

"I feel the same." She inhaled deeply. "After I lost Brad, I couldn't imagine loving another person or meeting someone as wonderful—in some ways, more so. I don't need to look any further."

He laid her on her back and leaned over her so that they were face to face, eye to eye.

"Marry me?" he asked. "Please, Maya Blackwood. Marry me."

"Yes. I want to be yours."

He held her tight. "You already are."

CHAPTER EIGHTEEN

Maya

The spring storm dumped five feet of snow on Blackwood. Maya was sure this meant that she and Kevin were deliciously housebound, but Kevin had his police radio and his home was hooked up to a generator so his laptop could display emergency activity.

To her disappointment but not her surprise, he showered and dressed for work.

"Where are you going?"

His smile had the ability to make her entire body tingle.

"Got to check on people." He adjusted his belt and clipped on his holster.

"How?" she asked, dumbfounded.

"Snowmobile. There are too many old folks that can't do for themselves. As soon as the plows roll, I expect I'll be shoveling, fueling generators, and all of the above in no time."

She rolled her lower lip forward. "It's not even daylight."

"It's my job." He leaned down and kissed her. "I'll get you a radio handset so I can keep in contact with you. For now, come here and I'll show you how to get a hold of me. Then you can go back to bed."

"I can't go to sleep knowing you're out in the snow in the dark." She threw off the covers and sat up. Kevin's T-shirt hung down her thighs to cover all her sexy bits. The bits that if uncovered could probably coax him back to bed.

"I'll be fine." He took his keys from the dresser and shoved them into his front pocket.

"I'll worry." She was terrified. Her husband had been traveling in the wee hours of the morning when he was killed.

"I know the town like the back of my hand. Remember? I drive these streets all the time. The snowmobiles have lights. It's all good." He held out his hand and pulled her to her feet and then into a hug. They stayed there for a long minute while she soaked in his warmth.

Moments later he led her into the living room, where he showed her how to operate the radio so he could check in with her.

"I'll be home for lunch."

"I'll cook you something." Keeping her mind focused on pleasing him would take it off losing him.

"I'd like that, sweetheart. And Maya…" He turned her so

she faced him. The soft touch of his thumb lifted her chin so she was forced to look into his eyes.

"Yes?" she asked, sounding sad that he had to go.

"I love you." He brushed his lips ever so slightly against hers. It was a kiss that promised more later.

She fell back to sleep curled on the couch with the fire roaring in front of her. There was no way she'd climb back in bed when her only way to get in touch with Kevin was the radio sitting beside her.

She woke to the smell of fresh coffee. Each night he set the coffee pot to brew automatically.

With the blanket still wrapped around her, she padded into the kitchen and poured herself a mug. Because he made it, it might have been the best coffee she'd ever tasted. She rolled it around on her tongue and savored the flavor. The radio hissed. Maya scrambled to answer it.

"Yes?" she asked.

"Hi," he said. "I'm checking in."

"Are you going to come home and let me make you breakfast?"

"I can do that, and then I have to leave again. One of our folks is an older lady who slipped on some melted snow. What she needs right now until I can get her squared away is a babysitter. She needs someone to sit with her." While the statement wasn't an invitation, she wanted to be helpful.

Without a second's hesitation, she blurted out, "I'll do it."

"You will?" he asked. "I wasn't asking, but that would be great."

"Of course, I will. I want to help." Deep inside, a feeling of purpose stitched her broken pieces together. Everything Kevin brought to her life seemed to make her whole.

"That's awesome. She's such a sweet lady, and she has no one."

"She has us now, doesn't she?" She topped off her coffee and leaned against the counter. The blanket fell to the floor but she didn't feel the chill of the morning air at all. All she felt was the warmth of Kevin's love. "I'll get dressed. Are you coming home for breakfast?"

"I'll swing by for something quick."

There was a moment of silence in which both of their minds went south for a second.

"You want a quickie?" she teased.

"You're killing me." The radio hissed and crackled. "I meant quick breakfast. I have oatmeal in the cabinet. After we eat, I'll take you over."

"I'll get it ready." She was already scouring his cabinets. She found the oatmeal easily and set it on the counter.

"Thank you, baby, for doing this."

"Anything for you."

She showered quickly and made breakfast the way she liked it. He had yogurt and frozen berries in addition to the oatmeal. She mixed the oats and yogurt and fruit together and let them sit until Kevin arrived. She topped everything off with brown sugar. When he walked through the garage door, she poured him a hot cup of coffee.

He stripped down to this underwear, leaving the damp

clothes by the door, and entered the house. She never tired of looking at him. Leaning against the counter, she took him in from head to toe. In the stark kitchen lighting, he was breathtaking.

"God, you're handsome."

He smiled, which only made her heart flutter and her core clench. She turned away to catch her breath and gain control over her hormones. All she wanted to do was strip down and take him to bed. When she turned around, she shook her head.

"You're with me all the time. When do you work out?"

"I work out while you're sleeping." He moved forward and took the cup of coffee from her hands. His chilled fingers brushed her warm ones. "Damon and I work out together. He comes over here or I go to his place."

"We need to work out together." She adjusted her sweater, tugging it down so it stretched over her curves. "I'd love to see those muscles in action."

He pressed against her, pinning her hips to the counter with his. He leaned in and whispered near her ear. "If you keep that up, poor Mrs. Jensen is going to get lonely."

She wrapped her arms around his waist.

"Then we should move it along." She moved aside, opened the refrigerator, and pulled out two bowls. "I made oatmeal my way."

He looked over her shoulder. "Is there another way to make it?"

"There's always another way. You know, variety is the spice of life."

"I'm a creature of habit, but it looks good." He was polite but without his normal confidence.

"You don't like it, do you?" She grabbed two spoons from the nearby drawer.

"I haven't eaten it. Did you cook the oatmeal?"

"No, the yogurt and the berries soften the oats. Let me zap it for you."

"That sounds delicious," he teased.

She laughed hard and butted up against him.

"Listen, if you don't like it, don't eat it." She heated the oatmeal for him and stirred it up, leaving the spoon in the bowl. "Taste it."

He took a spoonful into his mouth and smiled as if he was genuinely surprised he liked it.

"That's good." He loaded up the spoon and offered her some. "Eat up. It will take a lot of strength to help this old lady."

They hurried through their oats and bundled up to climb inside his truck. By now, the snow plows had cleared a path on the roads of the tiny town so Maya and Kevin could travel another way besides snowmobile. They drove over to Mrs. Jenson's house, which, like every other place in Blackwood, was close by.

Kevin knocked on the door and then turned the knob. He opened it a crack and stuck his head inside.

"Mrs. Jensen?" He looked at Maya. "She could be taking a

nap."

"I'm right here," said the woman, who looked like a frail Mrs. Claus.

Kevin stepped inside, pulling Maya behind him.

"Mrs. Jensen, this is Maya Blackwood."

The older woman gasped. "My word." She smiled at Maya like she knew her.

Maya turned to Kevin and made a face.

"She will keep you company while I work. Is that okay with you?"

"That's fine." Mrs. Jensen smiled. "That's just perfect." She waved Kevin off. "You go on."

The old woman patted the cushion next to her.

Maya looked around. The house was as neat as the geriatric homeowner could keep it, but it needed work. She decided there on the spot she would have Kevin do a walk around to see what needed to be done. She would also have a house cleaning service come in and help out. A coat of paint would be nice too if Mrs. Jensen would let her.

The older woman stared at Maya.

"Mrs. Jensen," she began. "Have we met?"

What started as a slow nod worked its way to an enthusiastic bobbing of her head. "I worked for your parents." The words were said with warmth and affection "Wait ..." She touched her finger to her lips in thought as if her earlier comment was inaccurate. "How about I fix you a cup of coffee and it will come to me?"

When Mrs. Jensen attempted to stand, Maya placed a gentle hand on her shoulder.

"I'll get it." Maya stood and looked toward the doorway that led to the kitchen. "Is the coffee already made?"

"Yes, I always have a pot on. It helps me stay awake for my shows."

She went to the kitchen in search of coffee. The space was as clean as could be, but the sight of the yellow kitchen with olive drab appliances confirmed what she already knew: Mrs. Jensen needed help in the remodeling department. She was living in the twenty-first century, cooking in a 1970s-era kitchen.

A moment later, Mrs. Jensen shuffled into the room and stood next to Maya.

"How do you take your coffee?"

"Black like my chocolate, dear."

"Me too."

She removed two cups hanging from beneath the cupboard and thoroughly rinsed them off. They were probably clean at one time, but now somewhat dusty.

"Now, let's sit and visit." Mrs. Jensen led them back to the couch. She got up one more time and returned with a photo album that was too heavy for her to carry.

"Mrs. Jensen, you should be resting. Didn't you slip and fall?" Maya asked gently.

"I'll be fine," she promised.

"We should have Kevin take you to the hospital in Idaho Springs to get looked at."

"I'll be okay." She pointed to the album. "Let's look at these."

Singularly focused, she cracked the ancient photo album open. On the first page were pictures of Maya's parents, her aunt and uncle, John, Caleb, and Patrick's parents.

"I used to babysit you all." Her smile stretched so wide the wrinkles above her lip disappeared.

Maya looked to the ceiling, climbing back in time. Her parents and John's parents went away often and left them behind. She turned to the old woman, who was sitting next to her, smiling.

"Oh, my goodness. You're her!"

Maya's phone dinged. It was Clem. This was perfect timing.

"Pardon me, Mrs. Jensen." She knew the older woman wouldn't appreciate a phone call in the middle of their conversation. Seniors didn't get the texting, social media, and five-second phone call habits of the younger generation. She would have bet her trust fund that Mrs. Jensen still wrote letters.

"Hey, Clem. How are you holding up? Do you need me to come home?"

"No. That's what I was calling about. Kaitlin is here. We're snowbound."

"Yes, I know." Maya immediately got his meaning. "Oh, you want to keep it that way?"

"Yes." His conversation was clipped, as if he wanted to get on with whatever he was doing. Maya's mind ran through all the options and she smiled. If Clem was happy to stay snowed in, it meant what was going on inside was more interesting than what was outside. This could be a positive turn of events.

"I don't want to keep you but guess who I'm here with." Her excitement couldn't be contained.

"I can't right now, Maya."

"Are you okay?" she asked, worried.

"I'm more than okay," he laughed. "Okay, make it quick. Who?"

"Mrs. Jensen. Our babysitter."

"Not ringing any bells."

"Okay, maybe later when you don't have someone else ringing your bell, you'll be able to focus. Have fun and don't get your heart broken again."

Maya hung up to find Mrs. Jensen taking her midday nap. She covered her with a nearby crocheted blanket and took a seat next to her. Maya closed her eyes for a few moments as well.

They both woke to the sound of a crew outside. Kevin and several rescue team members had been roaming the town clearing houses, checking on residents, and looking for structurally dangerous situations—things like hanging limbs and weighted-down wires. Spring snows were heavy and did a number on older structures. Clearing off the roofs, if need be, would not be a waste of time.

When they got to Mrs. Jensen's house, Maya and the old lady peeked through the curtains like they were two kids.

When the crews were finished and Kevin knocked on the door to take Maya home, she wasn't sure if she could bring herself to leave.

"Kevin, is she safe here?" Maya asked so Mrs. Jensen couldn't hear.

"Yes," he said with confidence. "We made sure. She's good. No gas leaks, water is good, sidewalks are cleared and salted. We did a total check."

"I want to say goodbye."

She walked over to her. "Do you need anything before I go?"

"I'm fine. You must come back so we can look at more pictures."

"I'd like that." Maya pointed to the table in the corner. "I wrote my number by your telephone."

"Thank you."

"Please call me. I'll bring you to lunch sometime or if you need to run any errands, I'll take you."

She hugged the woman while Kevin looked on.

As soon as they shut the door behind them, Kevin said, "I'm going to ask you to drive." They walked to his truck.

"Oh, you poor man." She gave him a good look and focused on the dark circles under his eyes. "You have to be wiped out."

"Dead on my feet."

CHAPTER NINETEEN

Kevin

By the end of the week, the snow had melted off the streets, but the mountains piled next to the roads would be there for a while.

Kevin stopped by the saloon to check in with Damon.

"Hey man. Why don't you come over to the house? We'll work out and have dinner. Maya will be there."

"That sounds domestic." Damon made a face as if to ask if what he heard was true. "You moving forward with her?"

Kevin smiled. "Yeah, I'm all in."

There were a few people at the saloon, but there was a guy at the counter that caught his eye. It was more intuition than anything else. Kevin checked him out in the mirror behind the bar. The guy returned his gaze and grinned a wicked grin.

"Maya," said the man.

It was the guy Kevin had tackled outside the meeting. Tim Johnson.

"Can I help you, buddy?" Kevin's jaw tightened enough to crush his molars.

"Not yet," smirked Tim. "But you will."

"And how would I be doing that?"

"As soon as my attorney gets a clearer idea of your net worth, I can answer that question with better accuracy. Since you're hanging out with a Blackwood, you should be rolling in the dough."

"Do you have other business in Blackwood?" Kevin grabbed the man by the collar.

"Kevin," cautioned Damon.

At Damon's warning, he released his grip.

"I'm buying drinks here," Tim replied. "Don't try to pin a loitering rap on me. Damon here is my witness. I think they call it unnecessary roughness."

"Wait a minute," said Kevin triumphantly. "Don't you have a history of alcohol abuse? Weren't you court-ordered to attend AA meetings? You aren't allowed to drink."

"Are you going to tackle me again?" he asked with a laugh.

"I might start with that but I've got more important things to do." Kevin didn't want to waste his time with Tim when he could be home with Maya. "Behave yourself."

"You too, and say hello to Maya for me."

Kevin grabbed the man again and escorted him out of the bar. Damon followed them.

"You can't do this!" Tim yelled. "I'm going to sue you."

"Already told you I'd love going to court. Knock yourself out, asshole." He guided him to the parked cars. "Better tell me which one yours is."

"I'll call the cops," he said. "I'm not kidding."

"I can walk you over to my office." Kevin chuckled. "You can speak with one of my colleagues."

Tim unlocked his car. "You're forcing me to drive with a few drinks in me." He gave him an evil grin.

"You're so right. Why don't you come on down to the tank and sober up?"

Kevin snatched him, weaving his arms through Tim's so that the belligerent man had no recourse. Kevin hauled him down Main Street, past the storefronts to the station. He had the attention of everyone on the street. Kevin walked the man into the station and sat him on a bench.

"You'll be more comfortable here." Kevin pointed to the pot of mud in the corner. "Want coffee?"

"You can't do this," Tim complained again.

"I can call the judge that ordered you to stay sober." He lifted a brow. "Weren't you looking at a good chunk of jail time?"

"You're a piece of work." Tim shook his head.

"Don't underestimate me," he said. "Sit there until you pass a breathalyzer. Then go home, and don't come back here."

Kevin had plans to drive up to Idaho Springs after his shift and pick out a ring for Maya. Instead, he had to babysit the man who attacked her. He gave it a couple of hours, but just as he was going to release Tim, the man's lawyer showed up.

"You holding him?" asked the lawyer.

"Not officially, no," said Kevin. "Not sure if you represented him in the matter, but he has a court order that prohibits him from drinking alcohol, and he was at a bar and professed to be drinking. I can administer a breathalyzer but then his alcohol consumption would be of record. It's your call."

The lawyer glared at Tim.

"He's been here a good while, but I can administer a random breathalyzer if I feel it is warranted."

A man Kevin didn't recognize entered the station with an envelope and placed it on the desk.

"Are you Kevin Hoisington?"

"I am." Kevin eyed the man with suspicion.

"You've been served."

The attorney and Tim smiled.

"Have a nice day, Officer." The lawyer escorted Tim out.

Kevin opened the package and read the complaint. Tim and his lawyer had indeed researched his net worth. They weren't going to get what they wanted, but Kevin started to calculate lawyers' fees and court costs. It would take a big chunk of what he owned, but he would live. Most important was that he didn't want them to get at Maya's assets. That meant he couldn't march her to the altar.

He'd wanted to marry her right away and now he

couldn't, at least until this was settled. To meld their assets would be financial suicide.

He thought of driving over to the Idaho Springs Hospital to see about having a late lunch with his mother, but she was at home because of the snow. Instead, he swung by her house.

One step inside and he was surrounded by home cooked love. Whatever she was making smelled fantastic.

"Mom, I'm here for a visit," he called from the front door.

"In the kitchen," she answered.

He wound his way to the back of the house, where his mother stood in front of the stove stirring a pot.

She turned and took one look at him. Mothers had a sixth sense about their kids. They always seemed to know when something was amiss.

"What's wrong?"

He let his head fall forward. "I was firm with a perpetrator and now I am getting sued." He took a deep breath and lifted his chin so he could see his mother's face when he told her the next bit. "Also, I've asked Maya to marry me."

Franny took a step back so she could look him in the eye. Her face was tight with emotion.

"I don't have to ask you if you're sure." She spread her arms for a hug. "I know you are."

Kevin leaned over so his mother could reach him.

"I'm sure. We both are. We want children, the whole nine yards."

They moved to the kitchen table as they usually did.

"Children," she squealed and then rubbed her hands together like she was planning a world takeover. "I can't wait."

"Calm down." With his palm horizontal to the table, he patted the air like he was settling it somehow. "Things aren't going as smoothly as I'd hoped, and I feel like I have to wait."

"Why?"

"This man, who I believe gets his income solely by finding people with assets and then gets his hooks into them, has targeted Maya and now me. I wanted to get married sooner rather than later, but I have to take care of this first."

"Kevin, you will wear yourself out if you try to make things perfect for her."

He chewed on that statement. "I was going to go to Idaho Springs and pick out a ring I think she'd like." His enthusiasm left with a heavy sigh.

"Kevin, if you want to marry her, marry her. Don't let this get in your way. If you do, he's won. Have you consulted a lawyer?"

"No, not yet."

"You don't even know if he has a case or not." She gave him a motherly pat on the hand. "You're standing here trying to solve this by yourself when you might not even have to. Where is she now?"

He looked at his watch. "Not sure, I can text her. Hold on a sec."

He texted Maya and got a quick response.

"She's at a meeting," he read and then looked at the time. "An early bird meeting whatever that is."

"She's going to meetings then?" His mother smiled. "That's a good thing."

"Yes," he said. "And you know Paula Jensen?"

"I do."

"Apparently she has pictures of the Blackwoods as children. She used to watch Maya, Clem and all of them when they were kids."

"That's a small world, but this is a small town." Franny rose to stir the pot.

"Yeah, but they were never around."

"Their parents weren't. I'm not sure why they kept the zip code because if I recall, the Blackwoods who lived in Lucy's house farmed their kids out to posh boarding schools and then lived on the ski slopes." She clearly disapproved.

"Let me get you something to eat. I made a pot of stew."

His mother's kitchen table was the same one he'd sat at when he was a boy.

"I'd love that, but I can't stay. I just wanted to say hi and see how you were doing with the snow."

He waited as she disappeared into another room and returned.

"Now Kevin, I know you have your heart set on buying Maya a ring." She held something in her hand and dropped it into his palm.

"But—"

"She can have it. I have one ring for each of my children. This one is yours." She kissed him on the forehead.

He opened the box to reveal a diamond ring. A sizable square diamond flanked by two smaller ones. "It's beautiful, Mom." His eyes stung with emotion.

"It was Grandma's. Maya can break it up and make her own ring if she likes."

"I'll let her know that." He stared down at the ring. The overhead lights sparkled off the stone, creating prisms of color that danced across the walls. "I have a feeling she would want to keep it the way it is. She's sentimental like that."

He let out a sigh, trying to release all the pent-up frustration he felt toward Tim Johnson.

"Don't let that fellow cloud your moment."

He nodded.

"You're right. I have to go. I'm going to make her a special dinner and give this to her." He closed the box and tucked it into his front pocket.

"When are you going to come over to my place and eat?" She pretended to sulk.

"When would you like us?"

"Anytime at all."

"I'll give you plenty of notice." He kissed her on the forehead.

"No need." She smiled. "I eat every night."

CHAPTER TWENTY

Maya

Maya and Togi sat together at the early bird meeting, enjoying a cup of coffee. They were now officially good friends and two people who supported each other. Maya hadn't increased her meeting attendance, but somehow, now that she was involved, it felt like she went to them more. Her life was rich and full, miles away from the life she led after Brad died.

She was zoning, half listening to the introductory portion of the meeting when someone sat next to her. It was Tim Johnson. She shook her head and gently nudged Togi. They both ignored him, though the smell of liquor seeping from his pores was hard to overlook.

"I sued your boyfriend today," he grumbled. He didn't get a response.

Maya didn't say a word. She knew she would talk to

Kevin about it later. She didn't have to rush to the rescue, but she turned and snapped a picture of him with her phone. She wasn't supposed to take pictures of people in meetings, so she suffered momentary awkwardness.

"Sorry," she said.

"Who you see here," he reprimanded.

"Shh." Maya and Togi picked up and moved. They sat in spots where he couldn't sit by them.

She didn't want to give this man the satisfaction of leaving, but if he kept being disruptive, she would have to. She would go to the station and see about filing a restraining order so she didn't have to deal with him at all.

He said something again from across the room and Togi leaned forward.

"Shh," she ordered.

"You want to hear the beginning stuff?" he mocked. "We hear that at every meeting."

"It's actually important, and if you listened to it, perhaps you would be sober," said Togi. "Please be quiet or take it outside."

"He's worth a couple mill." Tim continued to talk. "I intend to wipe him out."

Maya picked up and walked toward the door with Togi close behind. As she crossed in front of Tim, she turned and gave him a wicked smile.

"Then he'll have to live off of me." The ice in her voice chilled the air. "I will give him a nice big allowance. The right sponsor can do wonders for you, so find a man in the room and work with him." She lifted her nose into the air and inhaled. "You smell like a quitter."

As she left the meeting room, he followed her as he had before trying to continue their conversation.

"That allowance counts as income. I can make sure we attach that."

"Make sure all you want," counseled Maya. "You have to win your civil suit first. So far it doesn't look like you're capable of that."

She marched toward the station. If the man touched her, she would stomp on him with the heel of her boot. She wanted him to leave her alone.

"I'm going to the police station," she called out without turning and facing him.

"Kevin will have something to say about this," said Togi.

"Let him say something." Tim cackled.

It was then that Maya knew he was baiting Kevin through her. She dialed the Idaho Springs Police.

"Who you calling? Your *boyfriend?*" he taunted.

"Not quite. The officer in Idaho Springs to let him know you're stalking me."

Tim followed her and waited.

Maya dialed the officer's number and put Tim on video-phone so he could see him menacing her.

"I see him," replied the officer. "I'll dispatch someone right away."

Soon enough, another of the deputies emerged from the station. Tim darted to his car and pulled away.

"Thanks, Hal," Maya said to the deputy.

"We have his file and his license plate. Kevin had a run-in with him this morning."

"I want to go back in the meeting, but I'm afraid he'll come back and disturb it again."

"I'll stand out here." He set his hands on his hips and turned toward the street like a sentry.

Maya and Togi rejoined the meeting. After its conclusion, they walked over to the diner. She took a seat at a booth and waited for Kevin because she knew he would be there soon enough.

Togi went to get her an Arnold Palmer, and right on cue, Kevin showed up.

Maya didn't think she'd ever seen him angry, so she was guessing the intense look on his face was about as close as he got.

"Why didn't you come get me?"

"I didn't want to get you in trouble, and I didn't want to interrupt the meeting." She picked up her napkin, ready to shred it but set it down instead. "He was drunk."

"That's awesome news, because he has a court order that forbids him to drink, and if he's in a car, he'll get busted for drunk driving."

He leaned over and kissed her, and then slid into the booth across from her.

"I just saw, Mom," he said tensely. "She wanted to feed me, but I waited for you. Is Togi bringing you something?"

"Yeah. She's getting me a drink."

"Can we officially make this a date, like a dinner date, even if it is the diner?"

"I love the diner."

"I love you," he said intently. "I have something that might … just might make you feel better. I want to give you something that belonged to my grandmother."

He fished in his pocket and pulled out a diamond ring. It was so unexpected. Maya's heart melted. All the stress of the past hour was gone. Togi came back carrying Maya's drink, but as soon as the ring sparkled under her gaze, she set the glass down and disappeared.

He took Maya's hand, placed the ring at the tip of her finger. "Not sure if it will fit but we can get it resized if you like it." He moved from his side of the booth to his knee in front of her. "I thought about going into Idaho Springs and picking something out for you, but Idaho Springs, especially now, isn't the right place for us. This is your ring. If you want your own, we can do that too, but can we use this as a place-holder until then?" He stared up at her with love in his eyes. "Marry me, Maya."

Her eyes welled with tears. "Yes, the first time you asked, and yes this time, too." She was overwhelmed with the thoughtfulness of the man she loved and the sweetness of the ring. It was absolutely beautiful. It had an emerald-cut diamond with two baguettes on either side. Together they slipped it onto her ring finger. It fit like it had been sized for her.

"Imagine that, a perfect fit."

"How do you do that?" She knew he had no idea what she was talking about.

"What's that?" he asked with a twinkle in his eyes.

"No matter what the situation, you find the positive in it."

He nodded. "Much better approach than stress and anger, don't you think?"

She leaned forward and kissed him.

"It's beautiful," she whispered. "I don't want any other ring but this one."

He rose and took the seat next to her. "I'll never want another woman but you."

They sat in silence and stared at her ring. The ring that officially said she was his.

Maya broke the silence. "He said he's suing you."

"Don't worry about that."

Togi brought Maya a side of fries and coleslaw as if she knew Maya would need comfort food.

Kevin sighed. He didn't approve of her food choices.

Maya waggled her fingers for Togi so she could see the ring.

Togi gasped. "Congratulations." She gave her a fierce hug.

Togi even hugged Kevin.

"You should have a party at the saloon," Togi suggested.

"Not many people can brag that their sponsor recommended that," kidded Kevin.

"It's not a big deal. Besides, if she wants to get loaded, she doesn't need a special building for that." Togi glanced at Maya. "By the looks of her, you've got her drunk on love."

"That's a better alternative." Kevin covered Maya's hand with his own.

"I actually like that idea. In fact, I love the idea, and I love this town." She turned to Kevin. "And I love you."

"Then we can do that. Anything you want, baby."

When they were alone, he mentioned his mom again.

"Mom wants us to have dinner with her sometime soon."

"I'd like that." She lifted her hand and stared at the sparkling stones. "I want to thank her for my beautiful engagement ring."

CHAPTER TWENTY-ONE

Kevin

While Clem and Kaitlin were occupying John's house, Kevin invited Maya to camp at his place. He didn't mind having her there. It was so nice playing house with her. They were going to be married, so it was only a matter of time before she was there permanently.

From the last and probably final snowfall, there were big mounds of snow on either side of the roads around the town created by the plows that worked to clear the streets. Those mounds would remain for a long time, but otherwise, the roads themselves were completely ice free. The temperatures weren't dipping much lower than fifty, so the white mountains were melting at a good clip.

It was actually warm enough for Kevin to keep his garage open. He raised the door and backed his truck into the driveway because he, Maya, and his friend Damon were going to work out together.

Damon knew Maya, but they wanted to have him over so he could get to know her better since she'd be a permanent part of Kevin's life.

As he set everything up, Kevin acknowledged that his life felt so complete. He had such fun arranging the equipment. He knew Maya liked to jump rope, so he set up a cushioned floor he'd ordered for her to do that. She had had one at John's house she used all the time.

He dragged the weight benches so they were parallel for Damon and him. While he worked in the garage, Maya cooked. He loved that she was a homebody. She was downright domestic-looking in the apron she wore over her heart-stopping spandex workout wear.

The smell of whatever she'd made reached him all the way into the garage. He went into the house and sidled up behind her while she stirred a pot on the stove. His eyes dropped and walked all over her spandex-clad body. She was a damn wet dream to watch.

"What do we have here?" He looked over her shoulder into the pot. Whatever it was, it looked wonderful. It was more hearty than fancy, which said something about the woman who could afford caviar but preferred French fries and coleslaw.

He pressed his body to hers. He loved holding her. Loved that she was in his house. Loved everything about her.

She lifted a spoon from the pot for him to taste.

"Wow, that's delicious."

"Chili." She pulled the spoon to her mouth and licked off what he'd left behind. "So simple, and yet I thought it would be a nice post-workout meal. That and rolls and a salad. I made tea, but I'm not as good at it as Togi is."

"Hello?" called Damon from inside the garage.

"Hey. We're in here," he answered back.

Damon was so at home at his place that he just walked in. He was an enormous man, a fact which was more obvious when he wasn't behind the bar. He was larger than Kevin, wore all black that didn't diminish his size and carried a bouquet he handed to Maya.

"Thanks, Damon." She accepted the flowers. "You must have driven a distance for these. They're beautiful."

She put them in a vase.

Kevin and Maya fit nicely in his galley kitchen but Damon, who had been a defensive tackle when he played ball, crowded the area.

"This can simmer indefinitely," she said. "Let's go work out."

She turned the stove down to low and set the vase in the middle of the table and joined them as they headed to the garage.

"I was thinking about what we need in town and we didn't have."

"What's that?" Kevin prepared to spot for Damon.

"A gym." She said it like it was a big reveal with her hands spread wide like she was a game show host.

"I'm sure once the developers come in—if they ever do, we'll have one."

He counted as Damon bench pressed.

Maya jumped rope on the dance floor.

Kevin lifted the bar and put it back in place. "Wanna try?" He asked as Maya rested between sets.

"Sure, I'll go after Damon."

"Where would you put a gym if you could?" Kevin removed several weights from the bar.

"I thought we could put it in the town hall and make it free."

"The money would have to come from somewhere." Kevin dried his hands on a nearby towel.

"From a Blackwood, of course. I would pay for it. We could do after-school stuff. There's so much space that goes unused. I thought there was only one room—number eleven, but there's a bunch of unused space. Rooms one through ten aren't occupied. We could combine them."

"Insurance would be an issue." Damon moved to switch places with Kevin.

Kevin was suddenly self-conscious lifting in front of his girlfriend. She started jumping rope again, so he relaxed. Even though she wasn't paying attention per se, he pushed harder to show off.

"Okay, Bam Bam," chuckled Damon.

That got Maya's attention.

"Did you guys play together?"

"We played end to end." Kevin hoisted the heavy weights into the air. "He played after me."

"Why did you come back here?" She moved the rope side to side. "I mean, most guys do commercials or television or something."

He and Damon looked at each other and laughed.

"We like it here." Kevin wondered why she would ask.

"Yeah, we like it here," Damon mimicked. "I made enough to retire, and I work at my leisure. I have a paid-off house where I grew up. I'm set and I got it all before I got too hurt to be able to enjoy it."

"Did you get hurt?" Maya turned to Kevin with concern in her eyes. Her eyes skated his body as if looking for something she'd missed. "I mean, besides the helmet thing?"

Kevin lifted the pant leg of his sweats. He knew his scar wasn't obvious because he was so fair skinned and it curved perfectly around his kneecap. The surgeon had worked with such precision that it was nearly invisible.

"The helmet thing was a broken jaw and dental work that had my mouth wired shut for what seemed like forever."

Maya's scowl etched a deep furrow between her brows. "Not sure I could have handled knowing you then. There was so much risk." She rubbed the crease from her forehead. "At least you're not a cop in a dangerous town. I couldn't take that either."

"Blackwood has its moments," said Damon, smiling.

"Damon is my unofficial partner. He'd make a great cop."

"I'm happy where I am, thank you."

Kevin did another set. His muscles flexed and the blood flowed. Some stress that he didn't know he had released.

"You'll have to tell me some stories sometime." Maya finished jumping then picked up a weight to work her triceps.

The guys finished spotting each other with bench pressing and went on to curls on separate benches. When Kevin finished, he seized the opportunity to help Maya with her form. Not to improve it, but just to touch her.

He didn't want to be a spectacle in front of Damon, but he now thought of working out as a sexy endeavor.

"Anyone ready to eat?" Kevin wiped down the bench and bar.

"And police stories?" asked Maya.

"Sure." He winked.

They headed inside. He and Maya hit the master bath while Damon used the guest bath to shower and change before they ate. He had Maya sit at the head of the table while he sat across from his friend.

"This looks great," said Damon.

"Thank you." She blushed at the compliment.

"Did you make the bread?" Damon pulled his roll apart and dunked it in the chili.

"I did. What about you? Do you cook or do you take your meals at work?"

"I like to cook."

"I think most of the town is half and half," said Kevin. "Fortunately, the food at the saloon and the diner is good."

"I put the menu of the saloon together," Damon said. "I had to throw in a few Old West names but—"

"If you don't, people wonder why and if you do, the same," said Maya. "So, Damon, any significant other?"

Damon laughed and then stood up and took a bill out of his wallet and handed it to Kevin. "You were right."

"Told ya." Kevin tucked the money into his pocket and looked at Maya. "I told Damon when I invited him over you would probably bring up the subject."

"I'm not seeing anyone," Damon said. "I'm between relationships. Taking a year off for me, so to speak."

"Okay, I won't pry."

Kevin smiled. "But you want to, don't you?"

"You gotta stop." Damon laughed again. "I'm trying to swallow."

"I'm fine not knowing." She rolled her eyes.

"I'm happy for the moment," Damon said graciously. "If I feel like I need someone in my life, I'll be sure to let you know."

"This would be a good time to talk about cop stories or something else." Kevin took another roll and slathered it with butter.

"It's a shame about the town being sold and all," said Damon. "I like the idea of the community center. I'd love to be involved."

"I'm trying to change that."

"Maya wants to buy the town back." His chest swelled at the thought of his fiancée fighting for his town.

"Really?" Damon's face brightened.

"You haven't been fired, have you?" Maya played with her chili. "Togi says the people at the diner have been. She got a letter."

"No. I own the saloon, so no one bought me out." Damon set his spoon down and wiped his mouth clean. "If you look at Blackwood, my place historically was one of the first buildings erected. Back then, it was the most important. Gotta have our saloon, right? It's my building and then adjacent but not connected is the strip of shops I guess they built next. That's what got sold to the development company."

"You mean we asked you to sell and you didn't? We offered people a lot of money."

"You did, but I said no." Damon's voice was matter-of-fact.

"Did you know this?" Maya asked him.

"I didn't give it much thought. At least we know that we don't have to worry about that changing hands."

Maya wiped her mouth. "I have someone working on it, but I have heard nothing. We've reached out to the development company, but they aren't responding. It could be a long process."

Kevin helped himself to more salad.

"Deena didn't look like she was feeling too well. Maybe she should hand this project off to you."

"Yeah." Maya sat up straighter. "There isn't any reason why I couldn't investigate on my own." She stood up and kissed him quickly.

"I don't know." Damon tossed his wadded-up napkin into his empty bowl. "Maybe I should rethink this relationship thing. You're getting kisses and I'm not." He turned to Maya. "If you have a friend, I'm all ears."

Kevin laughed.

"Are you saying you like my future wife?"

"Ah, man." Damon's eyes opened wide. "Really? You two got engaged?"

Maya held out her hand. The diamonds sparkled under the dining room light.

"Congratulations. I don't know who to hug first. Do we have a date yet or is this all still too new?"

"I don't know when." Maya looked to him. "But I know we want to have the reception or some celebration party at the saloon."

Damon dropped his head and laughed. "That's perfect," he said. "We'll make that happen."

Maya clapped her hands. "I'm so happy."

"You know what we should do?" asked Kevin spontaneously. "We should go to the saloon. We should have a couple beers—or not—"

He looked to Maya apologetically.

"It's okay. I won't melt at the saloon."

"No, I'm sorry for suggesting we have beers. I forgot for a second."

"I can have club soda and I would love to line dance." Her smile was contagious. "That sounds like fun."

Everyone stood and cleared their places, leaving them in the sink to soak. Then he and Maya followed Damon back to the saloon.

CHAPTER TWENTY-TWO

Maya

The saloon was lively. There was another bartender behind the counter and a waitress. Kevin, Damon, and Maya went over to the pool table.

"Do you have dancing here?" she asked excitedly.

"We do." Damon put a quarter in the jukebox and music filled the air. Immediately a line formed.

Maya joined in, figuring it out as she went along, while Damon and Kevin moved to the pool table. She spied as Kevin racked the balls. Every so often their eyes connected across the room.

It was lovely to watch him in motion as she danced. He wasn't next to her as she moved, but it was like they were dancing together when they looked into each other's eyes.

She was lost in her adoration when Clem and Kaitlin pushed through the doors. Maya's face lit up. She hadn't spent much time with them since they'd reconciled, or at least were working on it.

Maya was so happy to see them together that she rushed to embrace them both. They quickly took a place at her booth while she put more money in the jukebox.

Across the room, Kevin's gaze was waiting for her. He gave a thumbs' up at her choice in music. He leaned against the wall, watching as she and her brother and sister-in-law lined up to dance. There were several regulars that snaked around, their bodies all going through the same motions.

She watched the game, wondering if she wanted to play as well.

Kevin leaned down and focused. He pushed the cue through his fingers and missed. He made a face, rolling his eyes as he looked to the ceiling.

Damon cupped his hands to his mouth and called out to her. She hurried over.

"It took you getting engaged for me to finally beat Kevin in a game of pool."

The waitress swung by and asked if Damon or Kevin needed drinks.

Maya noticed the way she looked at Damon then turned her focus on Kevin.

Kevin was oblivious to the attention. He only had eyes for her.

She walked him over to Clem and Kaitlin.

"Kevin," she said brightly. "You know the crew." He'd been there at the meeting so no one was a stranger.

Kevin shook hands with them but his eyes were still glued to Maya.

"How's it going, Clem?" he asked.

Clem looked at Kaitlin and smiled. "Things are good. Looking up."

"I was just telling these guys that we are engaged." Maya held up her hand and admired her ring.

Kaitlin and Clem looked up to Kevin. "Congratulations."

"Thank you." Kevin sat beside her, setting his hand high on her thigh. The intimate touch made her want to be anywhere but in a crowded bar.

They gave each other the look. The one that said they'd rather be naked and in bed.

"Are you ready?" She set her hand over his, then twined their fingers together.

"I am." He was ready to be alone with her. "It was nice to see you, but I'm about to take my fiancée home."

Stepping outside of the saloon into the chilly, peaceful dark, it felt like the world belonged to them. Blindly, she reached for his hand. They found each other, moving toward the same thing at the same time.

Kevin's body was like a warm coat against her, embracing her as their passion rose and melted the chill of the lovely Colorado night. She turned to him, leaned up against the truck, and wrapped her arms around him.

"I love you."

"I love you back."

"You've got to be the most grounded person I know. I

don't think you have an ounce of insecurity, and yet, you're not arrogant."

Just as she was describing his calm, reliable attributes, Kevin kissed her with a dark, ancient passion. The electric force of his affection brought her to the brink.

They rode quietly the few blocks to his place. He pulled into the driveway and killed the engine, but her passion was revving at full speed.

Maya and Kevin entered the house. It felt like she was walking into her house. It was a feeling she'd taken for granted. What she felt here, she couldn't name, but it was absent when she camped out at John's. She hoped that Kaitlin and Clem found something there that she could not.

She headed into his—their—bedroom as Kevin checked the windows and doors. Even in the peaceful, uneventful town, he swept the house every night before they went to bed, the same way he patrolled the town during his shift.

She was stripping out of her clothes when he entered the bedroom.

"Do you think someone will come in here?" she asked with a smile. "Does anything happen here?"

"Yes," he said plainly. "Look at the guy who bothers you at meetings."

She stopped and thought about it. She never considered that a possibility.

"Do you think he'll come here?"

Kevin lifted his shoulders in a half shrug, as if he couldn't commit to a solid answer. "He could, but I check everything anyway. I protect what's mine."

"Tell me a story with you and Damon in it and a bad guy," she said with a smile.

"Right now?" He closed in on her nearly naked form.

"No," she said breathlessly as he embraced her. "After."

She sank into his body, the hard planes of his muscles pressing against her softness. She loved the feel of her skin against him even if he hadn't undressed. He was big and solid, and so sure of himself. She lifted her face to his and found his soft, warm lips. She met his tongue with teasing strokes of her own. They twisted and tasted as their arms tightened. Kevin lifted her as he always did and it never got old. As soon as she was in his arms, her heart raced with impatience to be one with him.

While the universe hadn't necessarily always been kind to her, it had offered her the gold standard for men when Kevin appeared in her life.

He lay Maya down. Her passion-drowsy eyes savored the sight of him as he peeled his shirt from his magnificent frame. She grinned wickedly at the luscious vision. Ripples of muscles led to narrow hips and an ass carved from stone.

In seconds, they became a mass of tangled limbs. Arms and legs and mouths, scrambling and eager for each other. He nuzzled her, pressing his lips to the base of her neck as he moved inside her. She delighted in the fact that it was as if they were made for one another.

It was such sweetness as he loved her deeply and

completely. Maya's hands swam the broad planes of his back, feeling his muscles as they moved with each movement. He was virile, and powerful and hers.

Kevin's eyes were always fixed on her. When they made love, he looked into her soul. Any flaws and imperfections didn't matter.

Maya thought she would burst as they stoked their heat together. She closed her eyes as she felt her pleasure climb. She was as lost as she was consumed and dissolved into a quivering mass beneath him. Kevin moved with her until he followed her into ecstasy. Spent, they sank against the mattress, their bodies bathed in the light of their love.

Kevin drifted in and out of a light sleep while she lay wide awake. She lazily checked her phone when a text from Deena cropped up. The development company had responded. They were interested in talking with members of the Blackwood Corporation about buying the town back. Apparently, they'd bitten off more than they could chew.

"Kevin." She shook him gently. "It worked."

"What worked, baby?" he asked sleepily.

"I'm going to get the town back." It wasn't a done deal, but it was at least a possibility.

She settled happily into his arms.

CHAPTER TWENTY-THREE

Kevin

For two people with simple lives, Kevin and Maya had to make a date to finally have a dinner with his mother. Since he could remember, he'd had dinner with his mother at least two times a week but now with a girlfriend, he found he had to juggle things. For some reason, he was anxious about bringing Maya to his mom's house.

The night they were going to Franny's, he found Maya nervously primping in front of the bedroom mirror. She looked beautiful, but she was fussing over herself like she wasn't satisfied.

"Are you nervous?"

"Sure, but this too shall pass."

"So smart and so beautiful. If it makes you feel any better, I'm nervous too." He kissed her on the head.

"What?" She knitted her brow.

He knew she thought it was because of her. Not true. It was because even though Franny and he had a good relationship, it hit snags from time to time. Things didn't always come out the right way when she said them. Franny was a mom and sometimes that came without a filter.

"I want you to like my mom as much as I'm sure she'll like you."

She slicked on some gloss and turned to face him. "I like you and that's all that matters."

They headed out hand in hand.

The warm weather was holding, so they walked to his mother's house. The snow banks lining the streets had receded, giving them room to safely go on foot. It was a joy to hold her hand and take a leisurely stroll.

He hoped that nosy neighbors were peeking out the windows and noted that he was walking with his girl. All was perfect in his world.

Even with the snow on the ground, spring was in the trees. The snow hadn't kept the leaves from budding or the birds from singing.

"We don't have sidewalks in Blackwood, do we?"

"I don't know, Mayor Maya. It's not a sidewalk kind of town."

"I was thinking." She craned her neck to look up and down the street. "Maybe I'm getting ahead of myself, but I want to give back. You don't think sidewalks would be a good thing? It wouldn't change it much."

"I think working to get the town back is a way to give back to everyone."

"What if when I have ideas like this, once I get the town back, we could have meetings and ask people what they think?"

Kevin stopped and looked at her. "Now, that's a great idea. Selling the town and telling people afterward wasn't such a popular move. Keeping them in the loop is a better plan. Let's take it one thing at a time."

When they arrived at Franny's tidy rancher, they took off their shoes at the entry. Maya was uncomfortable walking around barefoot, but it was a Franny rule. His mom peeled their light jackets from them and hung them on the coat hooks hanging from the wall.

"Food smells amazing, Mom." Kevin bent over and kissed his mom's cheek. Something about whatever his mother cooked smelled like home.

Franny and Kevin had walked through a lot of craziness to get to that point, but they'd made it. Now both of their lives were even and peaceful.

"Yes," Maya said with a warm, friendly smile. "It smells incredible."

"Thank you," gushed Franny. "I hope you like beef." Her forehead creased with worry. "You aren't a vegetarian, are you?"

Maya made a face and smiled. "No."

"You're awful skinny. I was just wondering."

"Mom," scolded Kevin.

"It's okay. I am skinny. Been teased all my life with nicknames like string bean, toothpick, and stretch."

"String bean and Bam Bam." He winked.

He eyed Maya. Now that he knew her so well, he was certain she was more nervous than she led on. He rubbed her back to calm her.

"We can sit at the table," Franny said enthusiastically. "It's ready to serve. I like having conversations around a dinner table, don't you? We can eat and take it easy."

"Yes," smiled Maya. "That sounds wonderful."

Franny had planned out where everyone would sit. She pulled out their chairs until Kevin reached over her and drew the chair out for her.

He pushed everyone in and took his seat. Franny rubbed Maya's arm affectionately before she dished out the food. His mom wasn't a fancy cook, but a good one. She'd prepared beef stew and a green salad. It was reminiscent of the meal Maya made for Kevin and Damon. She had a basket full of rolls that Kevin knew she had baked.

At the far end of the table was a stack of photo albums. Franny was going to show Maya family and football pictures. She was bringing Maya into the fold one photo at a time. He smiled to himself.

"Any thoughts about when you will have the wedding?"

He noted that Franny gave Maya as much food as she gave him.

"Mom," he chastised. "She's not Damon."

"What?" asked Franny innocently.

He never knew if she was as clueless as she appeared or if it was her cover, but he never called her on it.

"Too much?" He pointed to the serving large enough to stuff a football player.

Maya nodded her head. "Yes, it's a bit too much."

He picked up Maya's plate and put some of it back. He knew her, she'd eat every bite so as not to offend and she'd hate herself for the rest of the night because she'd be miserably full.

"There you go," he said. "In answer to your question, we don't know exactly when we'll have the wedding."

"I know we want to have it soon." She looked at him with such love and devotion in her eyes. "I think we want it to take place within the next few months."

He took Maya's hand.

Franny giggled. She seemed beside herself with excitement.

"Good." She nodded.

"We're going to have the reception at the saloon."

Franny gazed at him with a blank expression and then shrugged.

"Is that a shrug of approval or disapproval?" He wasn't always sure with his mom.

"I like it. I know it's a saloon, but it's no different from the diner which serves beer too, so I'm fine with it."

"You know, Damon said that was the first building in town?"

"I guess so." Franny dipped her spoon into her stew and

pulled up a carrot. "People can't live without their watering holes." She took a bite and hummed.

"Mom, it's not just a watering hole. It's a gathering place. They dance there and they listen to music. Besides, my best friend owns the place."

"Did you all belong to a church here?" asked Maya, changing the subject on purpose. Better to talk about the ceremony than the reception at this point. "There is one church here in the town and then there are a few in Idaho Springs."

"What about John's house?" he asked. "It's roomy. There's nothing in it. It has a deck that runs all the way around it. That would be perfect. I mean, if you two agree."

"Actually, that's a great idea," Maya added.

Franny made a face or tried hard not to.

Maya explained. "My cousin John has this big A-frame house in the hills. It is a grand log cabin that he doesn't need since he married and moved. I've been staying in it. It has nothing in it but the bare essentials so we wouldn't have to move anything. It has big picture windows so you see the outdoors."

"Is it the place you stayed in right after Lucy left?"

The mention of Lucy stopped the conversation. Maya paused politely and smiled. Kevin cleared his throat and filled his glass of water from the pitcher Franny set out for them.

"Yes, Mom. That's the one."

"That sounds like a lovely idea."

It sounded like she meant it and wasn't just saying it to cover for her blunder.

"You and I can go over and you can see what I mean," Maya offered. "If you have a church in mind, we can check that out too."

"Thank you. It's nice that you're including me." Franny picked up the ladle and poured herself another helping. She looked at Maya's bowl but Kevin shook his head.

Maya giggled. "It's getting real."

"It was real the day I put that ring on your finger."

They both looked at Franny, knowing the ring came from her.

"Thank you." Maya held out her hand for Franny to see.

"It looks like it was made for you." Franny patted her hand in a motherly fashion and all tension left the room.

When their plates were empty, They leaned back in their chairs. It was more food than they were used to but neither of them was willing to not eat every bite.

"Would anyone like coffee?" asked Franny, clearing the plates.

"I'll get those, Mom." Kevin rose from the table.

"The coffee is made if you want to bring it out to us."

"Sure thing, Mom."

Franny walked over to the photo albums at the end of the table and looked at Maya.

"Would you like to see some pictures?"

"I would love to."

Kevin cleared the table and rinsed the dishes. He took his time joining the women. It was more fun to eavesdrop on them. The conversation was a different experience without him there. He took his time walking into the living room where Franny had moved them and sat in what used to be his father's favorite chair.

His dad had been gone for some time, but Franny was such a creature of habit and rarely sat anywhere else but a few select places—mostly at the kitchen table.

Kevin realized his hand was where his dad's hand had been at one time or another. He speculated as to how his father might like Maya.

As he looked at his mother and his fiancée, it occurred to him that he was looking at the future mother of his children.

She looked up from the photo album and caught him studying her.

He winked.

She blushed and returned her attention to the pictures. She let out an "aww" as his mother turned the page.

"What?" he asked.

Maya picked up the photo album and showed him a picture of himself in first grade.

"Oh, my goodness." She made her I-love-you face.

He laughed softly. Next Franny reached for the first of many football albums.

He held up his hand. "Okay, Mom."

"I'm interested. I want to see them all."

"Turnabout is fair play. Just wait until I get ahold of your photo albums."

"We might have to go to Mrs. Jensen for those," she teased. "My parents have passed."

Kevin was stunned. It was a major measure of how fast things had moved between them. He didn't know and he should have.

"I feel stupid right now."

He realized they never talked about her family besides Clem, and occasionally her sister Jennifer.

"Yes," said Maya. "Plane crash after a ski weekend. It took all the living senior Blackwoods. That's how me, Clem, Jennifer, John, Patrick, and Caleb inherited everything."

Franny nodded. "I'd read about that." She looked at her son and frowned. "I'm sorry for your loss."

"It was a while ago. In hindsight, I can't say it was a huge loss. They weren't around much. Us kids spent most of our time in private school and summer camp. You might say they never got over their youth. They valued their ski trips and their vodka."

She looked to both Kevin and Franny. Her eyes opened wide as if she'd figured something out. "They say drinking problems run in the family."

"They can, dear, but not always, if you're worried about Kevin."

"I meant me," she said with a laugh. "As always, I just realized my parents were both alcoholics. I wouldn't have thought about them that way before, but now I see it clearly. I was thinking I would have Clem walk me down the aisle. Franny, would you be willing to help me get ready? I'll ask Jennifer to be my maid of honor."

Franny nearly choked she was so happy. She wrapped her arms around Maya without saying a word.

"I'm going to ask Damon to be my best man."

"Do you think we should invite the whole town?" Maya tilted her head in question.

Kevin looked to the ceiling, not believing what he'd just heard, but there was no way he could say no. Maya had been alienated from her town, who was he to stop her from integrating into it now?

"Okay," he said easily. "I don't care. Sure, why not? We'll have the town over to John's and then a party at the saloon afterward."

"No, I mean to the reception," she clarified. "We can have family and close friends to John's and then everyone is invited to the saloon."

"That makes more sense." Kevin rubbed his hands together. "Deal. Wow, we are making some kind of progress here. I guess now we have to pick at least a time frame."

"Well … I've been talking to Deena. She thinks her morning sickness should be gone in the next couple of months. That will make ours a summer wedding."

"Then we should have it out back of John's house with the mountains as our backdrop."

Franny touched her lips as her eyes glistened with tears. God, he loved his mom.

But looking at Maya made his heart nearly burst. Soon. Very soon, she would be his.

CHAPTER TWENTY-FOUR

Maya

Since they figured they would have a summer wedding, Maya and Kevin decided they needed to have a version of a bachelor and bachelorette party. Maya called together all her female family members and friends. She invited her sister Jennifer, her cousins-in-law Lucy and Deena, Kaitlin of course, and her sponsor Togi.

She called Franny, but Franny declined.

"I understand, but is there something else you'd like to do? Do you want to help me with the menu? Damon said he'll make anything we ask for."

She liked that suggestion very much. She also said she would check out a few churches just so they had options, which Maya had to admit was not a bad idea.

Despite the bad memories of Idaho Springs, Maya took everyone to the spa at Indian Springs outside the town. She had a house there that had been empty since she'd cleaned up her act nearly a year ago.

When she announced the location, Deena admitted she was not feeling well enough to deal with the sulfur scent of the spa, so Maya had one fewer guest to consider.

She'd never canceled her maid service even though she hadn't been back to the place for all that time. It had been cleaned once a week ever since. For her guests, she had all the sheets changed on the beds and the refrigerator stocked. Outside of that, everything was set.

Togi and Maya went up ahead of everyone else. It was a strange feeling being in the house again. It didn't feel like it was hers.

There were a few things out of place and she wondered if the cleaning service had something to do with it. The shower curtain was torn where it hung off the hooks, like it had been yanked and she worried that maybe someone had been hurt while cleaning and had grabbed the curtain for balance.

That wasn't so weird, but there was a cigarette burn on her bedspread that caused her a moment of concern. Even when she was drinking, at least she thought, she never smoked. She didn't let people smoke in the house either. She would ask the service about it, though something told her it wasn't them. Otherwise, the place was perfect and ready for guests.

"Someone smoked in the house, Togi."

"Yeah?" Togi lifted her shoulders in a shrug.

"I must have been out of it at the end. It's so out of character."

"We usually are." Togi walked around the place like she was walking around the Ritz.

Maya had ordered a bunch of flowers to be delivered and placed them all over the house and in each bedroom. She and Togi picked up some last minute goodies at the local grocer —lots of chocolate.

She and Togi were the only nondrinkers, but Maya couldn't have alcohol around so she bought a lot of flavored sparkling water, which happened to be her favorite.

They hung out and waited for her other guests. When the ladies arrived, they headed over to the spa at Indian Springs. The sulfur springs were natural hot tubs. They each had warm mud wraps, facials, massages, and mani-pedis.

When they were all soft-skinned, relaxed and beautiful, she took everyone shopping at Eldora's.

Togi said she'd never been, so that was actually the first thing she put on her girls' getaway list.

"I can't," said Togi shyly.

"I can," Maya insisted. "You know I can. It's no secret. Why have it if I can't share? I want you to enjoy yourself. Get what you need or get what you don't need. Just get something."

Togi gave her a great big hug.

She looked around for wedding inspiration. She had the location and the time, more or less. Now she needed attire. She was looking at herself in the mirror at Eldora's, which like all the other shops in town, had an Old West motif. Maya suddenly saw herself as though she were back in time. Maybe when the building was new. In her imagination, the roads were dirt, ladies in lace and parasols walked through town. Wooden hitching posts were filled with tethered horses. Carriages carried families to the corner store to buy fresh farmed eggs.

"I have to have an Old West wedding," she blurted out.

She held up a blouse that looked antique. She summoned her sister over.

"Jennifer, what do you think?"

"Oh, my gosh, that's a great idea. One of the designers had a son who did that. It was so cool."

Of all the Blackwoods, Jennifer was the jet setter. She'd grown up realizing she had money and it made her feel better. She lived a pretty lavish lifestyle compared to the rest of the Blackwood children.

Maya envisioned her entire wedding. John's backyard rolling with mountain wildflowers, the bright blue Colorado sky. Kevin in an old-fashioned suit and a ribbon tie, and she in a gown with ivory lace. She fancied her hair in a messy bun.

She warmed with the idea. She would be married in her Old West hometown looking like the settlers might have.

Her great, great grandparents had settled Blackwood after they made a fortune on its gold, but the richness that she found was in the town itself and its people. She couldn't think of a better way to celebrate the love of the man she was going to spend the rest of her life with. It would be a fitting way to begin life there. If she got the town back, it would be like starting over from the beginning again, minus the gold rush.

"I think that's a great idea, Maya."

"Kaitlin, was I being insensitive inviting you? Where are you and Clem?"

"We're figuring that out." Kaitlin gave her a weak smile.

"I wish I knew if my mother had a wedding gown. I'm not sure I would fit it because I'm taller, but I kind of wish, you know? I can't remember, did you have a custom gown or was one handed down?"

"Clem has a lot of your parents' stuff in our attic back in Aspen. We could look. I had my mother's dress, but I thought some of your mom's things were there too." Kaitlin stopped cold and then closed her eyes. "I'm okay." She swallowed hard. "People go through things. Marriages go through things."

"They do," said Maya. "Hey, I can fly out there and look. Our plane is here."

"Why don't I see if Clem and I could go, if you don't mind?" Kaitlin made a mischievous face through her tears.

By the time the women got back to Maya's, they were wiped out. They gathered around the sofas and overstuffed chaises in their pajamas. She set tapas out and everyone ate at will. They were having a quiet and easy time when they heard what sounded like a key in the door.

The chain was on, so even someone with a key couldn't

get in. They braced themselves. She looked to Togi out of reflex, but she had no idea what was going on.

"Is this a bachelorette prank?" She glanced around the room to see everyone's faces, but they were all serious.

"I have a feeling it's not." Togi lifted from her seat like she was ready to fight.

"You call Kevin," Maya told Togi. "And Lucy... you call 911."

Everyone scattered. She decided she would find out who was trying to get into her house. Armed with her cellphone and a fireplace poker, she crept to the front door as a hand tried to reach around to undo the chain. She came down on the perpetrator's arm with the metal bar.

"Mother—!" the man cursed. She recognized Tim Johnson's voice.

Maya charged the door and closed it with her shoulder, slamming his arm again. He withdrew it with a scream. She heard footsteps running away from the scene.

The Idaho Springs Police sirens rang in the distance.

"I knew it," declared Maya. "I knew someone had been here. I cannot believe it. He's been staying in my house the entire time."

Maya wondered how the security company that operated the closed-circuit camera system hadn't alerted her. She shook with rage. When the spinning blue lights lit up the front of her house, she unlocked the door and greeted the police.

"We want to let you know we caught him," the officer

said. "He's in custody, but we have to take him to the hospital. Want to tell us what happened?"

"This man has been pestering her, that's what happened," Togi said. "He shows up everywhere she is, and I just happened to be with her. He tried to break into the house."

Maya nodded to confirm.

"I think he's been staying here." She shook her head. "I thought he was locked up for drinking."

"I'll have to look into that, ma'am." He took her contact information down and the names of everyone present.

That was it. She was going to sell her home in Idaho Springs. Except for visiting Lucy and John, she never wanted to come back to town ever again.

"Anyone want a house real cheap? Like free?"

"Is anyone else wide awake?" asked Lucy. "Do we want to stay here after that?"

Maya thought she would cry.

"Oh, don't be upset." Lucy attempted to calm her. "I thought since we got all beautiful and our guys are down in Blackwood at the saloon, we could crash their party."

Maya's phone rang. It was Kevin.

"Hold on, guys."

She walked into the guest bath.

"Hi, baby," she said.

"I'm coming up there."

"They caught him, and we're fine. We have a surprise for you."

"I'm coming up there." He talked to her with his no-nonsense police officer voice.

"Kevin Hoisington, no you're not. I promise you. Please trust me." She got him to agree.

It took a few minutes for the women to get ready. She packed up the food in a couple of the coolers and was going to instruct the cleaning crew to help themselves to the rest. They put on extra makeup and looked great when they cara-vanned back to Blackwood.

The filed into the saloon like they were the dancing girls invited to Kevin's bachelor party. They captured the atten-tion of the entire bar, which was open to the public. Kevin and the guys were at the pool table, his eyes immediately fixed on Maya as she led the line of women over to them.

"Hi." She leaned in and kissed him.

"Hi, baby." The tension eased from his face.

"Two pool tables, huh?"

"Damon bought another table just for the occasion."

"That was nice of you, Damon."

She walked over and gave him a big hug, then noticed her cousin Patrick.

"Hey, Patty." She hugged him next. "Better be careful going to a bachelor party. You could be next."

Patrick grinned. Maya thought he looked just like Caleb when he smiled.

"I know. Damon and I are the only confirmed bachelors left, I think."

"Yeah." Damon shook his head. "I'm not so confirmed."

"What's this?" Kevin asked. "Do my ears deceive me?"

"I'm thinking about someone." He looked between the two of them. "I see what you two have. I want that."

"Anyone I know?" Kevin looked around the bar, searching out Damon's love interest.

"No, I haven't met her yet." Damon's eyes scoured the bar like he was scoping out the options. "I'll let you know when I do. If only Maya had a sister."

"She does," said Patrick. "My cousin Jennifer is Maya's sister. She's right over there."

Damon followed their line of sight and found Jennifer talking to Togi. He waggled his eyebrows.

Maya and Kevin laughed.

"Do you have change for the jukebox?" She asked Kevin.

"I do." Damon hurried behind the counter and pulled out four quarters for each of the women who came to the saloon with Maya. He went over to the table they'd chosen. Lucy Blackwood came over to the men's corner.

"I'm just checking out the new table," she said eagerly.

"Hey," John said to Lucy. "Did you know Kevin played football?"

Kevin rolled his eyes and shook his head.

"Yeah," she said half-heartedly. "I knew that. You and I left town about the same time."

"How come I'm the last person to know anything?" asked John.

Maya put on a slow song.

228

"Here." Kevin handed his cue to Lucy. "Play my game for me so I can finally win."

He and Maya moved together to the dance floor.

"I'm so glad you're okay." He wrapped his arms around her and tugged her close to his chest. "I'm going to mess that guy up." Kevin was so level headed but there was no mistaking how upset he was about the events of the evening.

"He's behind bars, and we're here together. I'm so sorry for bringing all of this into our lives."

She thought twice about telling him that Tim Johnson had probably been coming and going at her place the entire time.

Kevin started to say something, but she put her fingers to his lips.

"This is the first time you and I have danced together, and I want to remember it for the rest of my life."

He held her close for the entire song.

She didn't tell him it was a song she and her late husband had danced to often. She held onto him, pressed her forehead to his shoulder and felt how healing and powerful love could be.

CHAPTER TWENTY-FIVE

Kevin

Kevin and Maya picked the middle of June for their wedding date. It was only a few weeks away. Despite all the business of putting a wedding together, he still checked up on the people of the town, especially the ones who needed him the most.

The biggest headache of the wedding—which was no big headache after all—was the fact that Maya had been looking for a wedding dress. She couldn't find her mother's dress so she ordered something online. She had just finished placing the order when she joined Kevin for their regular check-ins on her new favorite person, Mrs. Jensen.

Maya had arranged, with the old woman's permission, to make repairs to her home. She'd replaced all the appliances and put in a new kitchen floor. They installed a new roof and replaced the windows. The repairs were done in small stages so it wouldn't disturb Mrs. Jensen too much.

The remodeling gave Mrs. Jensen something to do. She and Maya visited and talked paint colors, floor samples, and appliance reliability. Maya seemed to love spending time with her. He constantly told her how proud he was for the selfless way she gave her time, talents, and money to others.

They stopped by often but today it was to check in and share lunch. Mrs. Jensen had been getting forgetful lately and they made sure she ate regularly. They also let her know they were getting married and that they were in the middle of planning the wedding.

"Well, now," said Mrs. Jensen. "That's fine."

"We were hoping you'd come," he said. "Would you like that?"

"I'd be pleased." Her face lit up. "I have something for you. I don't know if you can use it or not." Today seemed to be one of Mrs. Jensen's clearer days. It broke Kevin's heart that the woman he'd been looking after for years was slipping away.

"What's that, Mrs. Jensen?" asked Kevin.

"I have a wedding dress," she said. "It belonged to my grandmother. I've taken good care of it all these years. I was hoping I would have a daughter one day to give it to, but the only babies I ever took care of were someone else's. If you don't have one already, Maya, you're welcome to use it."

They were stunned and both sat at the table with their

jaws dropped. Kevin could not imagine what shape the dress might be in, but they had to indulge the woman.

"We could look, Mrs. Jensen."

"Well, then." She was up and moving down the hallway to her bedroom.

"Is there something I could help you with?" asked Kevin.

"Yes, dear." Mrs. Jensen moved well for a person her age but she was frail. Kevin followed her down the hall with Maya close behind. He dropped to his knees to reach under the bed where she said the dress was. He pulled out a beautifully made wooden box with a sliding lid on it and carried it to the living room and rested it on the coffee table so Mrs. Jensen could do the honors.

Maya's face transformed when Mrs. Jensen showed her the dress.

"Good?" asked Kevin.

"May I?" Maya's hands trembled.

"Yes," said Mrs. Jensen.

Maya pinched the garment carefully and held it up to her. The dress was a billowy, ivory-laced garment. Her eyes darted back and forth from him to the dress.

"What?"

"When I got the idea for an Old West wedding, this was the dress I had in mind." She held it under her chin.

"It's short." He looked down to where the dress ended at her shins.

"I would just add to it, but I think the rest of it will fit. Mrs. Jensen, it's beautiful, and it's in superb condition."

The old woman had a strange look on her face. She got up and walked over to the table against the wall. She pulled out a drawer and removed an ancient picture from it.

"This is me in the dress."

Something about seeing the young-looking Mrs. Jensen on her wedding day made him choke up. He looked to Maya, who had tears in her eyes too.

"My word, Mrs. Jensen," remarked Kevin. "You must have made your husband swoon."

"He loved me to the end." She looked at Maya. "I want you to have the dress. We can try it on and whatever mending needs to be made I could do it."

"I don't know what to say." Maya swiped at the tears tickling her cheeks.

"Say you'll take it."

Maya hugged her. "I will, Mrs. Jensen. I'll cherish it."

He did the lunch dishes as Maya tried on the dress just to see if it would fit. He had to promise to stay in the kitchen so he wouldn't see her in case it was a keeper. When he heard her squeal, he knew the dress was *the* dress.

Maya rushed around the corner from the living room to the kitchen.

"I'm going to stay here for a while." Her face was bright and beaming. "We'll work on the dress."

"Okay." He washed the last dish then kissed her forehead. "I have to patrol. Just give me a call when you want me to come back to get you."

He kissed her softly and thanked Mrs. Jensen. Before he

toured the town, he went back to the station. He monitored the status of Tim Johnson regularly. That asshole had surprised his soon-to-be wife and him too many times.

He knew Tim had an impending court appearance for what had become a stalking charge on top of breaking and entering. As that date approached, Tim's lawyer contacted Kevin repeatedly, trying to make a deal. If Maya dropped the charges, they would drop the suit.

Most of the emails went unanswered, but now that they were about to be married, he wanted to put the matter out of their lives so they would never have to deal with Tim Johnson again. He picked up the phone and called the lawyer.

"This is Kevin Hoisington. I have your emails and I'm turning them over to the state attorney. I'm no lawyer, but I'm thinking they would be considered extortion. My case has nothing to do with Maya's. You're a smart man and you know better than to make these demands. Do whatever you want." He added coolly, "Miss Blackwood has a restraining order against your client, and he was in her house. Consider the threats he made against her life. His presence would be considered a threat to her well being, do you understand me?"

"Are you threatening my client, officer?" asked the lawyer.

"You're proposing deals that make no sense, so I'm clarifying a few things so you won't be confused. I will appear in court for your civil suit if it doesn't get dropped, but if your client shows up anywhere near Miss Blackwood again, it will be considered a stand-your-ground situation. I say let the chips fall where they may."

He toured Blackwood after his call. He would be off in a week to put the wedding together with the help of some of his in-laws to be.

He got a text from Maya, telling him she was ready to be picked up from Mrs. Jensen's. He had never seen a more beautiful light in a person's face when he met her at the door.

"I wanted a dress that had meaning." Her voice tightened with emotion. "I can't tell you what that woman means to me."

He touched her hand.

"I wouldn't have met her if you hadn't been such a good example by helping others. She is one of the most important people in my life. I can't tell you how much I love you."

"I don't think I could tell you either," he said, choked with emotion. "But I will make sure you know, every day for the rest of our lives."

CHAPTER TWENTY-SIX

Maya

It was strange being in John's house after she had basically moved into Kevin's, which she thought of as theirs. Coming and going to the cabin felt exactly like it did when she came and went from a hotel. It was a beautiful venue but it was never her home.

Her life had come full circle. She had loved and lost and loved and won. There was nothing standing in the way of her happiness, including Tim Johnson who would be serving many years in prison for extortion and breaking and entering and a laundry list of other infractions. His record made it nearly impossible to file a credible suit against Kevin. They were free of him.

She'd known good men, bad men, and the best of men. The latter was where her future husband sat firmly along with her brother and cousins.

The guys had done such a wonderful job arranging the wedding venue. They built a simple trellis for Kevin and her to stand under and say their vows. With the weather expected to be spectacular, the chairs were set up out back in tidy rows for loved ones. She reviewed everything before she went upstairs to her former bedroom. Togi and Franny and some of the other women from town would be over soon to help her dress.

She heard an odd clip-clop which she knew was the unmistakable sound of horse hooves. She went to the nearest window to see what could make the sound. There, coming down the private road, was Clem and a man driving a horse-drawn carriage.

She thought for a moment she was imagining things. But no, she focused, and that was indeed what she was seeing.

The driver pulled the horse up to the far end of the culti-vated portion of the lot. John's property stretched hundreds of acres but only the most immediate section was landscaped with a conventional lawn. The driver stayed with the carriage as Clem came into the house.

He made his way up the stairs and into her room. "Like it?"

"Is that for us?" she asked.

"Yep. Better get ready."

Soon enough, all the special women in her life were helping her put on the dress she always imagined she'd wear when she married the man of her dreams. The plan was that the guys would make sure that Kevin was

KELLY COLLINS

distracted while she descended the stairs and met the carriage in the garage.

When all the guests had arrived and all the cars were parked and could no longer spook the horse, the driver pulled the carriage into the garage. Maya in her beautiful vintage wedding gown met her brother, who looked so handsome in his black coat and ribbon tie.

"I'll try not to cry." She tapped a lace handkerchief to her eyes.

"Me too." Clem thumbed his eyes.

They climbed into the carriage, whose only purpose was to whip around the landscaped lot and make a grand entrance to the wedding altar. The carriage stopped several feet behind the trellis and Clem helped her to the grass. He offered her his arm and together, they walked around the seated guests and up between them to the front of the aisle.

The guests stood while the bride walked behind her sister. It was a good thing that Clem lent her his arm because her eyes were blurred with tears. When they reached the altar, her brother took her hand and gave it to Kevin. He stared into her eyes with such love and devotion.

As Maya looked at the people surrounding her, she realized she'd come full circle. She'd arrived in her namesake town a stranger. She'd sold it off like it had no value. As she glanced at her guests, she realized that the value in the town was never in the structures, but in the people.

While it wasn't a done deal, in her heart she knew they'd

get the town back somehow and when they did, everything would be different.

Her eyes went to Clem, who looked longingly at his estranged wife. She hoped that they would find a piece of heaven of their own.

She turned to Kevin, who looked dapper dressed in black and white. He was a cross between lawman with his silver sheriff's star stuck to his jacket and outlaw with his devilishly handsome looks.

"You look beautiful, baby." He held both of her hands and looked to the minister as if to say *move it along*. He'd told her again and again that he'd been waiting his entire life for her.

"I love you," she whispered. For a brief second, she closed her eyes and thanked Brad for being a good man. She would always love him, but she wondered if he was all part of a bigger plan to get her to Kevin.

The officiant began. He spoke of love and promises and forevers. When he finished, Maya kissed her husband and knew her life had just begun.

A SNEAK PEEK AT NO REGRETS

Clem

The sweeping custom log home looking out on a field of aging wildflowers felt so empty. Even the majestic backdrop of the Colorado Rockies offered no serenity and it drove Clem Blackwood crazy to be there alone.

While his sister Maya had fallen in love, married, and moved out, his marriage to his childhood sweetheart, Kaitlin, was on a downward spiral headed for the end. Clem had a lot to think about, too much time to think about it, and a great big beautiful empty house to think about it in.

He had a constant mental war about his soon-to-be ex. Whether he loved her or hated her, he couldn't decide. It seemed like she had the same problem. Sometimes she didn't want him around, but when he left, she followed.

Luckily Clem had a new project to occupy his time. His friend Damon Perry, who was also the owner of The Blackwood Saloon, had set up a gym in a space at the town hall. It was the first and would probably be the only one in the small town named after Clem's family.

The enterprise had been Damon's brilliant idea. He'd been a pro football player and was something of a small-town hero here in Blackwood and wanted to create a place where the community could gather for healthy endeavors.

Clem wanted to help, though helpful was the last thing he was as he sat on a weight bench drinking a cup of coffee and plucking an imaginary daisy that always ended with, *he loves her.*

He could have hit the ceiling when another one of his sisters, Jennifer, and his estranged wife Kaitlin waltzed in dressed in spandex that should have been against the law. Filled with lust and frustration, Clem tried to remember the last time Kaitlin wore anything like that for him. Now that she was on the way to being single, did she have to look so hot? If he closed his eyes, he could almost feel his hands brush over her lush curves. He let out a low growl and sipped his coffee.

Their relationship, for all its confusion and miscommunication over the last two years, was always on-track in one department. Clem had never lost his physical attraction for Kaitlin. There was something incredibly powerful that transpired between them. The arced sexual energy they tossed back and forth was as powerful as a lightning storm. She was open about feeling the same way, but it confused him when she expressed how unfulfilled she was. In his mind, he filled her just fine.

After fifteen years, their smooth and seemingly happy relationship had hit a wall of discontent that Clem couldn't wrap his head around. He didn't get it. They had everything. Money. A beautiful home. Cars. Vacations. Right now, the one thing they didn't have was each other.

Most frustrating was that Kaitlin left him and now she'd chased him to Blackwood from their home in Aspen.

He watched her walk in and take a look around the gym. Her eyes lighted on him several times and when they did, there was heat in them.

His body remembered the last time they'd fallen in bed together in what he thought was make-up passion, only for her to waffle about her commitment to their marriage.

As much as he wished he was happily married, the way he'd thought he would always be, Clem was done with Kaitlin's back and forth. He had to draw the line, but as he laid eyes on her again, his heart ached for what could have been. He wanted it all back. The good. The bad. The hot sex. It aggravated him to no end that he'd get one stop closer and fall two steps back.

While he worked hard at accepting the demise of his relationship, she had to show up looking so damn good that it made his balls ache.

He sighed in resignation. The awful truth was that he missed her. Loved her and wanted her back.

He shook his head and counted to ten while his way-too-handsome gym partner smiled from ear to ear.

"Ladies," greeted Damon, oozing too much charm.

"Hi," Jennifer nearly purred. "We're here to work out."

"What else would you be doing in a gym?" snapped Clem. "We don't serve tea or sell shoes."

Kaitlin faltered between a smile and a frown. "Can you show us how to work the equipment?"

He set his coffee on the ground and grabbed a dumbbell he'd been doing curls with. "You go like this," he said sharply, rigorously pumping the weight.

Kaitlin walked over and touched his bulging bicep with her fingers.

"Ooh," she said. "The gym had been kind to you."

"What are you wearing?" Clem asked Kaitlin with two full helpings of irritation and a spoonful of desire.

"Clothes," she snapped back.

Fortunately, Jennifer and Damon didn't catch that Clem had just been an ass, but Kaitlin did. She always saw him at his worst. Her face crumpled as though he'd told her she was ugly.

He could have kicked himself, but he couldn't stop. He continued his lecture.

"You're lucky Kevin isn't here. He'd arrest both of you for indecent exposure."

"I'd say what is exposed is pretty decent," joked Damon, suddenly listening.

"Don't encourage them." Clem curled the weight until

strain etched his features.

"What do you want to do?" Damon asked as if scolding a child. "Discourage them? Come on, you two, let's all get along."

Clem was in agony. The last thing he needed was to be seeing the woman he used to sleep with strut around with her amazing body clad in an outfit that might as well be a second skin. *What was she thinking?*

He watched her interaction with Damon to see if her intent was to impress him. All the while, he reminded himself that she had her own life to live. He got that. It was clear, standing so near to her in the gym, that Blackwood was way too small a town for the both of them. He couldn't bear witness to her moving on from the marriage.

He liked Damon, but if his ex-wife had designs on the ex-pro baller, Clem couldn't stick around and watch it. He was selfishly relieved when his sister Jennifer flirted with Damon and he reciprocated.

The second he figured out that they had a thing going, he immediately decided they looked fabulous together. He would jump through hoops to support that blooming relationship.

Jennifer, at 5'8", was not the tallest of the Blackwood women, whose average height approached six feet.

Damon had to be near 6'3" and a massive wall of muscles. His tawny skin resembled the Blackwoods, but he wasn't related.

Jennifer looked like she could take a walk down a

runway, and Damon wasn't too far from magazine worthy himself. With the sparks flying between them, they were definitely on their way to being an item, if they weren't already.

Much to his relief, Clem had been jealous for nothing.

When he checked out Kaitlin again, she was touring the equipment that the small gym offered. She lifted a lighter dumbbell than the one he'd used, but it was still heavy for her size.

Clem thought her form could use a correction. He knew he should leave it alone because he was agitated, but staring at her in Spandex pulled him closer.

Kaitlin was in such great shape that people ridiculously assumed she came by her figure naturally, which was not the case. He knew she'd worked at it her whole life. While the smart thing to do would be to leave her alone, he wasn't always so smart. Besides, she wasn't used to free weights and she could genuinely get injured.

"You're going to hurt yourself, baby." His voice softened with the use of an endearment she always loved.

"Show me, then." Kaitlin handed him the dumbbell.

He expected her to be upset that he'd butted in, but she seemed amenable to his instruction. He set it down and selected a lighter weight.

"Here." He wrapped his arms around her then moved her arm, loaded with the weight, up and down. "Like this."

They watched themselves in the wall-to-wall mirror. Kaitlin's eyes met his in their reflection.

Clem felt himself transform. His gaze grew dark and focused as she smiled at him with silly, mock adoration. From the moment they'd first met till now, Clem thought she was the most beautiful woman he'd ever seen. He was certain that would always remain the case. He wouldn't care if Kaitlin was fat, skinny, bald or gray. She would always make his heart race with her presence.

He loved holding her in his arms. The fact that she had moved out and their marriage was failing was even more painful. Instead of being grateful that she let him put his arms around her, he snapped at her again.

"Look, if you aren't going to be serious—"

"Oh, I'm completely serious," she said with an ear-to-ear grin. "What's this do?" She put down the free weight and moved away from him toward the lat pulldown.

"That's loaded up for Damon and me. Let me adjust it for you."

Kaitlin was goofing around. She used her body weight to pull down the bar. It was too heavy for her and she released it. It all happened so fast. The bar snapped back wildly and headed for her face. She got winged just a bit but missed the full force. A little nick bled on her cheek.

Clem raged. "What the hell were you thinking?"

Everyone was stunned by his thunderous voice.

Tears glistened in Kaitlin's beautifully made-up eyes.

Clem just now noticed her hair and makeup was not what a person wore if she was serious about working out. She looked more like she was trying to attract attention. *His.*

Finally, she spoke. "That's a good question," she said quietly. "What was I thinking?"

Clem was sure his yelling hurt her worse than her near-miss with the equipment. Her cut dribbled and a blue ring developed around the tiny wound. He felt like an idiot.

It was time for a softer approach. "Let's look at the cut on your face." He leaned forward and thumbed the tiny spot of blood from her cheek.

"I'm fine," she said, brushing him away.

"We have a first aid kit."

"I'm sure it's not that bad." She looked at herself in the mirror on the wall. She appeared surprised.

He stooped down to catch her gaze, which she averted so she didn't have to look at him. He regarded her with a sincere expression, filled with sorrow and regret.

"Hey," he coaxed gently. "I'm sorry I've made you mad, sorry I hurt your feelings, but we should look at that. It's starting to bruise."

"He's right, you did get hit in the face," affirmed Damon. "Do you have a headache or any of that?"

"No," she said cutting her eyes away from them. "But I have a pain somewhere else." She glared back at Clem.

Damon laughed but gave her a look of sympathy.

Kaitlin turned to Jennifer. "I'm going to wait in the car."

"Did you bring a coat?" asked Clem.

"I'm not cold," she said with a sternness that would make a nun blanche.

"I'm just trying to be nice."

"I'm not interested, okay, Clem? It's a little too little and a lot too late. Just leave me alone."

Even in the horrible moment, Clem had to laugh at Kaitlin's stubbornness.

"Baby, it's October in Colorado. You can hate me if you want, but I'd hate to see you hate yourself when you're shivering and freezing that fine ass off in my sister's car."

He went over to the peg where his hoodie hung. She shivered at the door but let him put the jacket around her.

"Jennifer, I'm driving her home." The serious tone of his voice left no room for argument.

"Okay, she's at my place," his sister said. "My new place. Our new place. We're roomies."

Clem turned to Jennifer, slack-jawed.

She threw up her hands like he was making a big deal over her announcement. "I found a place. Decided to put down some roots here." She looked at Damon. "At least for a while."

Clem turned to Kaitlin. "You aren't living in Aspen and just visiting?"

"No." She pointed to Jennifer. "I'm living with her." She lifted her head in defiance but Clem knew his wife well enough to know she was on the verge of tears. They were collecting in the corners of her eyes.

"Okay," he said with heaviness in his heart. "I'll take you to Jennifer's." It nearly broke him to know she would be so close and yet so damn far away.

GET A FREE BOOK.

Go to www.authorkellycollins.com

ABOUT THE AUTHOR

International bestselling author of more than thirty novels, Kelly Collins writes with the intention of keeping the love alive. Always a romantic, she blends real-life events with her vivid imagination to create characters and stories that lovers of contemporary romance, new adult, and romantic suspense will return to again and again.

For More Information
www.authorkellycollins.com
kelly@authorkellycollins.com

Printed in Great Britain
by Amazon